Henry Lawson Hero of the Robot Revolution.

Henry Lawson Hero of the Robot Revolution by Robert Denethon
2nd Edition
Book I of the Henry Lawson Hero of the Robot Revolution Series.
A Socialist Unrealism, Australiana Noir, Speculative Faction,
Bushpunk novella.
Robert Denethon is a 'nom de plume'.
Copyright © 2011 Submariners Map Imprint Western Australia,
An imprint of Submarine Media Pty Ltd
Malaga Western Australia 6090
ISBN 978-0-9923681-1-1
submarinemedia@eftel.net.au

I0659197

Never let the truth get in the way of a good story.

Mark Twain.

Somewhere in the mystic future, on the road to Paradise,
There's a very pleasant country that I've dreamed of once or twice
It has inland towns and cities by the ocean's rocky shelves,
But the people of the country differ somewhat from ourselves

....Henry Lawson

AUTHOR'S DEDICATION:

FOR MANY, TO ONE

R.D.

Contents

THE PROTAGANIST(LAWSON)'S THANKS AND DEDICATIONS.

Many thanks are due to Bertha for allowing me to use her diaries as a source, particularly for the voyage to Marx Zealand and certain other sections where my memory was not perfectly reliable.

To Robot, Andrew Barton Paterson, Harry and Hannah, without whose assistance nothing would have been accomplished.

Introduction

THE PAMPHLET

'Freedom in a Land Girt By Sea'
1907.

"Midnight Knock"

'So the shearing shed, complete with sheep in
it, is burning to a cinder, and I'm riding through
the bush looking for the German Unionist who had
set it alight less than two hours before. It is
half past midnight, the desert air is brisk and
cold and I see a faint light over the rise - a
campfire, smoke ascending, the smell of lamb
roasting. Three troopers are riding a little way
behind me. Billy, the aboriginal tracker, leads
us onward slowly. "Just over the hill, boss. One
cove, at campfire; looks like Hoffmeister."
'I say to the troopers, "Aye, lads, take care
now. Go quietly. That German bastard is just
over the rise. And I would say he'd be eating
one of Dagworth's lambs, thievin' bastards, those
Unionists. Daly and Dyer go round. Cafferty and
I will come in right at him. Won't be nowhere but
he can go, except into the billabong, and he won't
do that if he values his immortal soul. Stay here,
Billy, no reason for you to get involved."
'I go over the rise with Cafferty and Dyer and
Daly go around.
'Hoffmeister is bowed over the campfire,
stirring a billy of tea. A treebranch is hanging
over the fire with a lamb roasting on it. The
firelight flickers on his face.
'I said, "Who do ye reckon that lamb belongs
to, Hoffmeister? You're the bastard that burnt me

shearing shed - and here ye are, got the cheek to
eat one of the few lambs of me flock that wasn't
burned to a crisp, in the fire YOU started. Ye'll
be comin' with us, Hoffmeister, to Waltz the
Matilda right the way to rot in gaol forever, you
thievin' Union brandisher."

'Hoffmeister stands up, looks this way, looks
that, sees that he's surrounded, and I'm thinkin
he really will jump in the Billabong.

'He opens his mouth and we all think he's about
to say, "You'll never take me alive," 'cause that
was always his boast to his mates.'

'The men who occasioned the Union pub in
Barcaldine told me afterwards they heard him say
it a million times if they heard him say it once.
"Those squatters will never take me alive," he'd
say, brandishing his rifle, his bravado fueled by
a few shilling's worth of cheap Union beer. "I'd
kill myself before I'd let them take me," he used
to say.

'But in that very moment in which he is about
to commit suicide by trooper the moon comes out
from behind a cloud - was that what changed his
mind? The moon reminded him a'his girl, perhaps?
Who can say? He goes limp and drops his rifle and
says, "Take me in. I will not resist. It was me
who burned your shearing shed, Macpherson, and it
was a deed that will not bear any good fruit, I
would warrant." Who can say why he decided not to
do himself in? I wish he had've. It would've been
better for every one.

'So we took the bastard back to Dagworth then to
face justice.'

Bob had finished his tirade.

'Really, Bob, what you did to him wasn't
justice,' said his sister Christina. Bob frowned.

Andrew Barton Paterson turned from the window
to face Christina, and said, 'You came out,

Christina, and took charge, or so I hear.'

'I was waiting for Robert to return,' she said, scowling. 'They'd beaten Hoffmeister to a pulp and tied him to Robert's horse and made him run behind it. By the time they got back to Dagworth he was black and blue and bleeding, with a fractured arm, a broken toe and a few missing teeth.'

Bob strode out, slamming the door. Christina said, 'He doesn't want me to tell you.'

Paterson leaned casually against the piano and wrote something in his notebook. Christina was seated primly on the sofa in front of two cups of tea, a teapot, silver sugar spoons and an elegant sugar bowl arranged neatly on a tray on the sofa table.

'I think there might be a poem in all this, or at least an article for the bulletin. So, when Robert arrived, you wouldn't let them continue tormenting Hoffmeister.'

She adjusted her spectacles and tried not to notice how good-looing Andrew was; he was much too sophisticated for Christina. A little too fond of the hard liquor. Then again, he did come to the Presbyterian Church on the Sabbath on occasion when he was up in Queensland. Christina thought he might be talking with their pastor about his drinking, but she wasn't sure. Perhaps the accident that had happened when he was twelve, that had withered his arm, gave Andrew an excuse to drink, but Christina didn't think that much of an excuse, in any case.

He didn't let his slight disability stop him from being involved in tending the horses and riding with the other men, though there were limitations. Perhaps it's why he had become a solicitor, an occupation he clearly despised.

It was his habit of writing poetry, however, which had led to his engagement to Christina's

best friend Sarah Riley, for he had written her a
lovely poem, "Eyes of Blue." He wrote Australian
bush poetry, much of which had been published
in the Bulletin, and there were even rumours of
a book. Sarah Riley disapproved - she said his
writing 'distracted him from the task of becoming
a full equity partner in the firm.'

But now his engagement to Sarah was all off,
and Christina wondered if he could possibly be
interested in her.

'The Banjo,' as the men called him, smiled at
her in a slightly rafish way and she found herself
feeling hot under the collar and avoiding his
gaze. Thoughts of him kissing her, touching her,
caressing her, came into her mind unbidded, and
she sighed a little and almost surrendered her
soul to them, almost leaned against him and put
her arm around him. She pursed her lips - these
were unacceptable thoughts.

'You took charge, Christina?' he said.

'Oh, I'm sorry... my mind wandered... Yes
Andrew, I took charge. Billy came running in,
saying, "Ross is beatin' up a white feller, miss,
as if he was one of us!" I had earlier told Billy
to come to me if anyone mistreated the blacks
on our land - I would give any man short shrift
who did, Andrew, even Robert. Because of Billy's
warning I was awaiting them when they arrived -
you should have seen the look of shame on Robert's
face when he rode in with that poor German fellow
being dragged behind the horse, and realised that
I was there.

'Hoffmeister was a mess. The first thing I did
was to make sure that his broken arm was set
properly, and then I tended to his wounds. I've
not treated a man that badly injured, not since
that nasty old fellow from Rockhampton molested
one of the maids in '92 and the shearers gave him

a hiding.

'This time it was only sheep and a shed that Hoffmeister harmed - mere possessions - despite all the bullets that were flying around, the only person hurt was one of the roustabouts foolish enough to stick his head up at the wrong instant, and he woke up again five minutes later. We can buy more sheep, the shed is insured, but a human being is far more valuable. I can't understand why they cannot see that their treatment of Hoffmeister only increases the gulf between the unionists and the squatters? I cannot see how a reconciliation can be achieved now. I only foresee more Union troubles, for many years to come. And the more intransigent the Unionists become, the more intransigent the Pastoralists' Association becomes also. I fear that it may result in bloodshed; a civil war, before the turn of the century.'

Andrew flicked a dust particle floating in the sunlight. 'I've been working both sides, Christina, to try to bring about a reconciliation. Robert is big in the Pastoral association.'

'The other squatters respect his opinion, particularly on financial matters.'

He was Scottish. Andrew chuckled. 'A joke, Christina, you ought to watch yourself. You might find that you're enjoying yourself.'

Was that what he thought of her - someone who could not enjoy herself?

It must have shown on her face, for a faint shadow passed over his expression. Was she too prim and proper? Goodness gracious, our religion ought to be one of joy and gladness, not rules and regulations - that's what George MacDonald would say - a Scottish author of whom Robert wouldn't approve. Robert was all rules and regulations, no dancing, read the scriptures on the Sabbath, don't

do this, don't do that, blah blah. Blow him. She
would do as she pleased.

She undid her hairclip and placed her
spectacles upon the tea tray. Her hair fell
about her bosom, and she loosened the neckpiece
on her high-necked dress slightly and sat more
comfortably upon the sofa, revealing the tiniest
amount of flesh upon her ankle.

'Goodness gracious, Christina,' said Andrew,
suddenly beside her on the couch. He caressed
her cheek gently and then rested his hand next to
her thigh, a feather-light touch. A hot flush went
into her face, and a strange shiver ran through
her. She closed her eyes.

Suddenly he took her hand, smiled and winked
at her. 'There is a woman under all that clothing
after all,' he said sardonically, and embraced her
and kissed her, full on the mouth!

She found herself returning his kiss with
a passion that surprised her, and he began
unbuttoning her blouse.

◊ ◊ ◊

The trial of Hoffmeister took place the
following month. Andrew, being only a solicitor
and not a member of the bar, could not act for
the accused, but Mr Street, Andrew's employer,
travelled up from Sydney with the especial
intention of acting on Hoffmeister's behalf. A
Union fund paid his fee, which was unusually high.

When Andrew arrived, one of Christina's
maids was in the stalls beside her, weeping
disconsolately.

'Emma seems to have had a bit of a fling with
Hoffmeister,' said Christina, smiling warmly
at Andrew and thinking about their fling. 'Poor
girl,' Andrew whispered poignantly, 'Those other
fellows in '91 got six years just for planning
sedition. What will they give to Hoffmeister, when

17

he actually did something?'

The trial lasted five days. The jury, decidedly weighted towards pastoralists, was not sympathetic.

Billy summed it up after the trial, when told the result. 'White man's justice - put a fellow in a big hole and leave him there till he rots away. That's the difference, Miss Macpherson, between white and black here in this country. If a black fellow should kill a white man, black fellow won't last long - he'll be shot or hung up from a tree pretty shortly. But a white man kill a white fellow, he might get mercy from the judge, or he might not. He'll be out of gaol in ten years, maybe, if his neck's not in a noose. But a poor white fellow do something to a rich white fellow's property - that's when they treat 'im even worse than a black man.'

Hoffmeister was given twenty-five years in gaol for attempted murder for his part in the attack on Dagworth, plus another fifteen years for the damage to the shearing shed, to be served concurrently. Even some of the squatters commented that it was an extraordinarily harsh sentence.

They dragged Hoffmeister away in chains to the watchhouse. He was shouting gibberish; he appeared to be losing his mind. Emma watched silently, and Christina and Andrew feared for her mind as well, for she appeared to be 'in catatonia'.

He was transported to Rockhampton later in the week, to do hard labour.

Emma sobbed disconsolately day and night. Christina made sure there was someone to accompany her for every hour of the day in the following weeks, for she feared the poor girl might attempt suicide.

♦ ♦ ♦

Christina and Andrew were married a month later - the church gossips labelled it a rather hasty engagement - and their first child was born early in the next shearing season, but their happiness did not last for long.

Andrew wrote this article for the daily newspapers at the start of the civil war in December of 1895:

BARCALDINE, FRIDAY: The men, fired with a passion that has lately been seen all too often in these parts lately, and bearing firearms to the very last man, were baying for blood. There has been no shearing anywhere in the north since the start of this season. Since the execution of Bennett and Prince at the behest of the Governor the mood among the men has steadily worsened. But the name that brings forth the loudest shouts from the Unionists is the name of Hoffmeister.

The Unionists' leader, William Hamilton, recently freed from gaol again by the Governor in a futile and rather feeble attempt at appeasement, addressed the Union Camp at two thirty in the afternoon. He was standing in front of a tiny memorial sapling, recently planted in ashen ground.

'We must never forget the first tree of knowledge which was burned to ashes by the squatters. But knowledge is perennial - we have planted a new tree of knowledge, to symbolise the new knowledge brought to our shores from England in the writings of Karl Marx, the immortal author of Das Kapital. He wrote in German!' How the men cheered; they were cheering for Hoffmeister more than Marx.

'Just as we ought never to forget the Paris Commune, as Marx says, and all those who have died at the hands of Capitalists, so we ought never to forget the names of those who have suffered the deprivations and humiliations of unjust imprisonment and torture at the hands of Capital in Australia. Smith, Barry, Fothergill, Forrester, Stuart, Taylor and Griffin, and the two Murphys. And those who died -

Blackwell, Brown, Prince and Bennett... And those who still suffer under the rod of oppression... Samuel Hoffmeister!' The crowd cheered even more for Hoffmeister, for a living martyr to a cause is an even greater hero than a dead one.

'Samuel Hoffmeister still rots in gaol; a sign of this Australian land which still aches and cries out, for she is still bound in the chains that Mammon has laid upon her! Samuel Hoffmeister is a symbol of the suffering of the poor, the worker, the downtrodden at the hands of the rich and comfortable! We must fix the rotten heart of Australia, and the place to start is the Town Hall in Barcaldine. Behold the earth is red, for it will flow with the blood of the squattocracy, and then the land will be purified! Blood must be spilled in return for blood!'

The roar of the crowd was terrible, and the author of this article wishes that he never had to see such a sight again, but fears that he will, for the evil is upon us now. To a man the Unionists rose up, firing their guns into the air and crying aloud, and it was as though an unclean spirit had taken hold of the entire crowd and was working its insane will through them. Like a baying mob of desert dogs they came forth at the Town Hall, crying out for blood. Though the wooden doors were battened against them, even the strength of hardened mahogany could not stand against such force of numbers. The doors cracked and the mob breached what feeble resistance the Town Councillors and the constabulary could put up, but the poor men were dragged bodily out of the hall, screaming aloud and bleeding profusely from their wounds.

On this day they were executed in front of the aforementioned sapling.

On this sad day the blood of the Town Councillors and the local constabulary, the blood of their fellow Australians, watered the roots of the new Unionist Tree of Knowledge in Barcaldine. One wonders what became of the philosophy of mateship. This is a sad day for any who would call themselves Australians.

◆   ◆   ◆

Several weeks after this incident, at midnight,
Christmas eve, 1895, in fact, the Paterson family
- Christina, their first child Harry, and Andrew
- made ready to flee Dagworth station, for the
civil war had all but reached their doorstep.
Christina's brother Robert stubbornly refused to
leave, insisting that he would defend his property
to the death. He was deaf to all of Andrew's pleas
and reasoning, to his own detriment.

Andrew, driving the two horses, and Christina,
carrying baby Harry, sat upon the small cart that
held their meagre possessions as it hobbled slowly
down the track for the last time. Billy met them
at the front gate of the station.

'Miss Macpherson,' he said, 'There is a big
Union mob coming here, all riding on horses. They
already took Kynuna station, Miss Macpherson,
and nobody knows where Miss Riley is, and the
station's all burned down. There aint nothin' left
of it. You better get out of here. Nobody knows
what they might do next, Miss Macpherson.'

'Billy, it's Mrs Paterson now. I'm married to
Mister Paterson now.'

'I know. An' my name's not Billy either, Miss
Macpherson. Look at you, Mister Paterson - all
packed up and ready to go! But when they meet yer
on the road, it won't be 'G'day Mate,' will it,
Mister Paterson? How did you know the Unionists
were coming, Miss Macpherson?'

'The telegraph wires were still up when they
attacked Kynuna, and they sent us a message, so
we got ourselves ready.'

'Nobody there now to send you a message. Me
and the mob will look after you, Miss Macpherson.
You just head past those flat top hills down near
where the telegraph wire goes along the railway
line, and we'll find a place to hide you and Harry

and Mister Paterson in the bush there. After all,
you always looked after us - stopped the boss from
beating us and whenever someone was sick, you
come to give em medicine. Me aunty'll meet you
there; you keep an eye open for her and she'll
have some dinner ready for you and you can just
stay in one of our places for a change. Arks
her for anything you want. But we don't have a
piano, that's all, but we got everything else.' He
smiled. 'You can see what's it's like living like
a real Australian.'

'Why are you doing this for us, Billy?' Andrew
asked. 'You don't owe us anything. We have done
little enough for you over the years.'

'Miss Macpherson, she looked after my nephew
when Mister Macpherson wanted to flay the skin
off his back just for havin' a sheep for lunch. An
wivout her medicine, me aunty would've died. Now
we're going to look after you.' Another black man
came out of the shadows.

'This is my nephew. Me and him, we're going
to take your cart along the road to Kynuna and
they'll think it's you ridin' it. You take them
fast horses, Mister Paterson, that's all yer need,
leave all yer stuff behind on the cart, you take
the quick horses and we'll go get some other ones
and tie them up to the cart.'

Later on this decision to leave their
possessions behind was something that Andrew
often said saved their lives.

In the camp that night, Billy told them what had
happened while Andrew and Christina were riding
south towards the flat-topped hills, and Billy
and his nephew were riding Andrew's cart up the
Kynuna road.

Billy and his nephew had met the Red
Revolutionary Army on the track. 'What have we
here?' the leader of the rebels had said, firing

his gun into the air, as a band of thirty or forty
armed men surrounded the little cart.

One of the other revolutionaries, a red-headed
chap, had said, 'They're blacks, Willy, leave
them alone.' Another said, 'Looks like they've
taken the Macpherson's cart. They're thieves.
Shoot 'em.' But the leader had laughed and said,
'Why should we care if they take the Macpherson's
stuff? Let them go. Let them take whatever they
want. The squatters won't have any stuff any more
pretty soon.'

Christina asked Billy if he knew what had
happened to Robert, but he wouldn't say. All he
would say was, 'Nothin left of Dagworth, Miss
Macpherson.'

   ◆ ◆ ◆

After three months of living with the mob,
Andrew said to Billy, 'Thankyou for everything
you have done for us, please thank everyone in
the mob. It's time for us to go. The towns Back of
Bourke have been secured by the Red Revolutionary
Army, and the commanders appear to have taken
their forces eastwards to the coast to take
Rockhampton. This is the time for us to go south.
Perhaps Melbourne will not fall to the Reds.
Perhaps we can make a new life there. Thankyou,'
and Andrew used Billy's real name.

They fled south through the outback, across
the border, through the bush and into the Blue
Mountains; a bitter-sweet journey, for the
peaceful country that spawned The Man From
Snowy River was fast disappearing, destroyed by
violence, class rivalry and bloodshed.

They took refuge in Melbourne, but the rebellion
moved south almost as quickly as Andrew and
Christina fled, and soon there was no free place
in Australia left in which to hide.

   ◆ ◆ ◆

After the final victory of the Red Revolutionary
Army, the declaration of the Republic of the Free
and the foundation of the new capital city of Marx
in the Australian Capital Administrative District
halfway between Sydney and Melbourne, Andrew and
Christina assumed other identities and went into
hiding. His prior journalistic efforts had made
him a prime candidate for a new kind of Union Camp
in the north - that bore the label of Mateship
Indoctrination Camp, a peculiar oxymoron; the
kind of literary expression the Reds are adept at
producing.

In those camps the most advanced science of
the twentieth century is being used even today
to alter the unacceptable social opinions of the
intransigent Bourgeois elite - in other words,
those who have the courage to resist are tortured
mercilessly until they either recant or die.

On the 12th of February1904, Andrew Barton
Paterson, his wife Christina and their three
children were asleep when a knock came at the
door at midnight. Andrew Paterson disappeared
on that day, and it is not known whether he
still lives in some outback Indoctrination Camp,
breaking stones under the hard sun, or whether he
has died who so many others who were sent to the
desert.

But in those pockets of freedom that still exist
in the outback villages and the private homes
of independent thinkers, Andrew and Christina's
songs are sung. To this day one particular
prophetic song defines the lost dream of a free
Australia for those who do not wish to be part
of the revolutionary status quo; the haunting
melody that Christina based upon a Scottish
tune, Craigielea, for which Andrew "The Banjo of
Freedom" Paterson wrote the words:

BY ROBERT DENETHON

<u>Waltzing Matilda.</u>

Oh there once was a swagman camped in the billabong
Under the shade of a Coolabah tree;
And he sang as he looked at the old billy boiling
Who'll come a Waltzing Matilda with me?

Who'll come a Waltzing Matilda my darling?
Who'll come a Waltzing Matilda with me?
Waltzing Matilda and leading a water bag,
Who'll come a Waltzing Matilda with me?

Down came a jumbuck to drink at the billabong
Up jumped the swagman and grabbed him with glee
And he sang as he shoved that jumbuck in his tuckerbag
You'll come a Waltzing Matilda with me.

Who'll come a Waltzing Matilda my darling?
Who'll come a Waltzing Matilda with me?
Waltzing Matilda and leading a water bag,
Who'll come a Waltzing Matilda with me?

Up rode the squatter, mounted on his thoroughbred
Down came the troopers Onc Two Three!
Who's is that jumbuck you've got in your tuckerbag?
You'll come a Waltzing Matilda with me!

Who'll come a Waltzing Matilda my darling?
Who'll come a Waltzing Matilda with me?
Waltzing Matilda and leading a water bag,
Who'll come a Waltzing Matilda with me?

Then rotted the swagman in a tiny dungeon cell,
'Till one day there dawned The Republic of the Free,
Now a knock comes at midnight on the intellectual's door,
You'll come a Waltzing Matilda with me...

Editor's note - the strange spelling is intentional, a result of the 1898 spelling reforms in the Socialist state. It is only used in the introductions and chapter headings and in one or two places in the text.

KARAKTERS:

Henry Lawson ('Harry')

The Direktor

Bertha Lawson

Robot

Mister Tohunga

Henry Sutton

Andrew Barton Paterson

Professor Dominica Rossum

Hannah Thornburn.

REVOLUTIONARI UNITS OF KONVENIENS:

DIVISIONS OF KURRENSI:

The Revolutionary Pound = 100 shillings

The Revolutionary Shilling = 100 pence

The Revolutionary Penny = 1 pence.

DESIMAL DIVISIONS OF TIME:

The Day contains twenty Ours.

Each Our contains one hundred Minits.

Each Minit contains forty Sekunds.

An old minute is worth 55.555555 new Sekunds.

THE DAYS OF THE TEN DAY WEEK:

Wunday, Tooday, Threeday, Foorday, Fiveday, Sixday, Sevenday, Ateday, Nineday, Tenday.

THE WEEKEND:

Sevenday to Tenday.

BY ROBERT DENETHON

<u>NAMES OF REVOLUTIONARI LOKASHYUNS:</u>

GLORIOS REVOLUTIONARI KOMMUNITITAT OF MELBURN
= City of Melbourne

NAMES OF REVOLUTIONARI ORGANISASHYUNS:

FRATERNAL AUSTRALASIAN REVOLUTIONARI KOMMUNISTIK UNITED AL-
LIANSE
= the Communist Party - the sole political party in the
democratic system of Australia.

THE RED REVOLUTIONARI ARMI
= the army that took the cities of Brisbane, Sydney and
Adelaide and declared Australia to be the first Communist
Republic in the world. ,

FREE REPUBLIK ESTABLISHED AS KOLLECTIVITI IN AUSTRALYA
= the official name for Australia today.

MARX
= the capital city of Australia.

MATESHIP INDOKTRINATION KAMP   (M.I.K)
= a Union camp where people are re-educated to become
good citizens of AUSTRALYA.

CHAPTER 1.

POET OF THE PEEPL RITES GLORIOS REVOLUTIONARI PROPAGANDA

Take life one heart-ache at a time. That's what I eventually learned - it's the only way you can get through it. If you look ahead too much, you get yourself into trouble thinking about things that will never happen; good and bad things. And if you think too much, you tie yourself in knots.

God made us very simple, it says in the Good Book, but we made ourselves very complicated. But Robots were made complicated from the start.

But I'm getting ahead of myself. Let me start at the beginning.

It was Ten O-Klok noon on Wunday in G.R.K Melburn and I was at work on a propaganda leaflet.

The Direktor of Publik Literatur's bald head glinted in the light and his tiny, round, professional looking spectacles magnified his eyes to enormity. He turned to me and said, "Have a good weekend, Mister Lawson?"

"Yes." What else can you say to a Direktor?

He waved a pamphlet in my face.

"Mister Lawson. This pamphlet is the one we want refuted in your next publication. A typical example of the scurrilous Anti-Revolushyunri propaganda coming out of the Anarkists these days. Rats, hiding in their hidie-holes from the Guvernment. I'm sorry, it's rather hard going - uses the old speling..." He handed it to me.

The pamphlet was printed on butcher's paper, and appeared to have been reproduced using a lithomimickograph machine. The type quality was even worse than the pamphlets we printed, but it was still legible.

I looked it over. "I haven't seen this one before."

He grabbed it from me again and flipped through it, looking for a particular page. "It contains an interesting detail - you remember that reactionary poet, Andrew Barton Paterson? Well, it appears he might have named his first child after you, Mister

Lawson. Harry... That was your nickname, was it not, in the days of the Bulletin?"

A cold breath of fear went down my spine. Was he fishing for information? Had I become a person of suspected Unakseptibl Politikl Tendensees, after being held up as an example of Marxian heroism for all this time? But the intensely fervent expression he wore when he was denouncing someone was missing. I was still persona grata, for now.

I replied honestly, "Yes - Harry is short for Henry. And yes, Direktor, that's what they called me in the old days. Though I haven't any clue as to why he might have named his first child after me; you see, we had quite a falling out a year or two before that. Paterson was a bit of a dark horse, though; he had a sardonic manner. You never knew what he was thinking."

The Direktor turned the pages and pointed to this passage in the middle of the pamphlet -

...at midnight, Christmas eve, 1895, in fact, the Paterson family Christina, their first child Harry, and Andrew, made ready to flee Dagworth station...

It was strangely moving. I wouldn't have expected Paterson to have named his dog after me, much less his firstborn son. But there - you never know with people, do you?

I said, "Anything else, Mister Direktor?"

"Not for now, Mister Lawson."

"Well, I'm taking this with me to the park so I can read through it whilst I have my pipe. Alright?"

"That's fine, Mister Lawson. The others have to follow all the rules, but, Marx bless you, you're a Hero of the Revolushyun; you are A Trusted Mayt; you are one of the Fabyulus Foundas of F.R.E.A.K.IN Australya! Why, you have a higher Sekurity Kleerans than anyone in this office except for me, and that is certainly saying something, Mister Lawson. So go right ahead."

So I left the office taking my tobacco pouch, my pipe and the pamphlet.

On the way to the park one of the Invisibles, those poor

devils in rags with haunted eyes that hang around the rubbish bins and alleyways in the worst parts of town came up to me and grabbed my arm as I went past, pulling me roughly into the alleyway.

His clothes stank as though he hadn't washed for weeks.

He shook my arm more than a Sydney barman making a cocktail and shouted, "They're alive you know. Alive! They think and feel like you and I do. Trapped! Trapped inside! They're human!" I thought he was talking about the poor unfortunates in the Re-Education Kamps, but he pulled me closer and whispered in abatoir-reeking breath, "The Robots. They're alive, Mister Lawson. They. Are. Alive."

I turned away from his rancid breath, wrenched my arm loose and sprinted off.

He must have been a recent release from the Kamps. The Kamps send them insane, if they don't die in there. An accursed business, but you can't make an omelette without breaking eggs, or at least, that's what I once thought...

I wonder what would have happened if I had queried him a bit more about the Robots? Perhaps things might have turned out differently, but I doubt it. Things tend to go wrong anyway in life, no matter what you do.

Ten minits later, I was sitting under a eucalyptus tree in the HENRI LAWSON POET OF THE PEEPL REVOLUTIONARI PARK cutting up a pipeful and watching a willy wagtail chase an old crow away from his nest.

I lit my pipe, took the pamphlet out of my shirt pocket and began reading.

CHAPTER 2.

A RAW NERV

Well, if you've read the Introduction you already know what the pamphlet said - you know it was nothing much - typical reactionary propaganda. It treated Banjo Paterson's last days on the station with Christina, and that famous incident at the waterhole (and Banjo's poem, Waltzing something or other) and then a few months later, the Revolution. But I had known a lot of the people mentioned in the pamphlet personally, Banjo, Archibald, Christina, even Hoffmeister the shearer, and somehow it seemed to touch a raw nerve.

I got a bit teary. I missed the old days. Alright, back then I had no money, I spent nearly every waking moment boozed to the eyeballs, and I suppose everyone saw me as a bit of a hopeless case, but the thing is, I had mates - Archibald would do anything for me - gave me that train ticket to get out of Sydney and see the bush - and they treated me kindly, even Paterson with his sardonic sneer - indeed, any one of them would lend me a quid for a beer, even before midday. Back in the days when midday was called twelve-o'clock, and they used to talk about 'the yard-arm', too, though what that expression meant escapes my recollection.

Now my mates were all gone, taken off to the Mateship Re-Education Kamps. And the coves that were left were only nice to me because they were afraid of me. They all pretended that everything was fine, that their friendship was all voluntary - but I saw the fear in their eyes. I saw the misery on their faces when they thought nobody else was looking. And I fancied I could hear them groan whenever the Publik Announcement began at Seven O-Klok every single day, though I knew that was ridiculous, unless they were groaning very loudly. My government issue hearing aid was just not that good.

The crow was definitely getting the worst of it, and flew off resignedly, and the willy wagtail flitted down and picked an insect off a fallen banksia cone then returned to his nest to give it to the young ones with his little tail twitching proudly.

It struck me that the crow could stand for the EVIL KAPITALIST PIGS and the willy wagtail could stand for THAT HEROIK UNDERDOG, THE VIKTORIOS AUSTRALYAN WORKER. I nodded to myself - once I had the seed of an idea, my work was as good as done.

It was just hack work, though. I couldn't call myself a poet any longer.

This afternoon I would walk back to the Truth-Bulletin offices and write my blog, then retire to the public bar at half-past thirteen to drink free beer until I was completely blotto. Such was the reward that the FRATERNAL AUSTRALIAN REVOLUTIONARI KOMMUNIST UNITED ALLIANSE liked to bestow on all the Heroes of the Revolution.

Not much of a life, really. But I'm telling you about it so you know how it all began - so you realise what my life was like before I became the Hero of the Robot Revolution.

BY ROBERT DENETHON

CHAPTER 3.

BERTHA LAWSON, FED UP WITH HARRI'S UNKONTROLLABL ALKOHOLISM AND THE INTRUSIV, UNIPRESENT PRESENS OF THE ROSSUM OMNIVERSAL ROBOT, INFORMS HIM THAT SHE INTENDS TO LEAV HIM AND APPLI FOR A DIVORS.

Coming home after midnight is vague in my memory. How I got there I don't know. Suppose I stumbled through the streets, took a nap in a gutter, then wandered along until some taxi driver recognised my face from all the statues and, figuring I might be sober enough to remember his face if he didn't, took me home and deposited me on Bertha's front doorstep without charging.

I remember walking in, though. That was unforgettable. The Robot was standing at the door waiting for me, and his metal joints creaked as he took my coat. "Let me assist you sir; the movement centres of your brain appear to be temporarily impaired; in all likelihood the effect of some sort of liquid intoxicant."

Bertha was standing in the kitchen doorway, staring daggers. "It went to the door and waited for you a good five minutes before the taxi arrived. How did the Robot know you were coming then, Harry? Tell me that? How did you know, tin man?" Suffering from paranoia, I thought to myself.

The Robot ignored her and guided me to my lounge chair.

"Let me get you a glass of water, sir - it may help to mitigate the worst effects of alcoholic dehydration."

"See?" said Bertha, "Even the Robot knows you're a bloody drunk. You're an alcoholic, Harry. You've got a problem, and you refuse to face up to it!"

The Robot stood beside me, watching as I finished the water. It refilled the glass from the pitcher it had taken from the refrigerator - I suppose it knew I was drunkard. It wasn't the first time I'd been out most of the night, and I would have wagered it wouldn't be the last.

"God I hate that thing," she said, tapping its head as though it was a tin can. "While you're at the pub it stares at me the whole time, Harry, I'd swear there's someone in there, inside that metal head, looking out like a little man from one of those guard towers they have at the Aerostation to stop people from escaping blanky F.R.E.A.K.IN Australya."

"What do you mean?" I was slurring even those few syllables. "It's just a bloody mashchine, Bertha. There is nobody in there. Nothing in that iron skull but cogs and wheels." But I glanced up - those disconcerting eyes - so similar to human eyes and yet distinctly unlike them - I remember thinking, perhaps she was right. It did seem as though there was a person lurking in there, looking out, peering at the world he wasn't able to participate in. "You're bloody imagining it, woman," I said, trying to convince myself that she was. "I thought I was supposed to be the one with the big *imagination*."

Bertha replied, "What an imagination! Churning pamphlets out faster than the Robot factory makes tin men."

I laughed bitterly. Propaganda was not my true calling. Poetry was my calling, but I had lost the heart for that years ago. Honoured by the world my words had helped to make, I had lost my soul. I looked up - the machine looked back at me with soulful eyes, mocking my lack.

"Oh, Harry," Bertha sobbed, twisting around to look at me, "Don't you see? I can't take it any more. I can't live here any longer - with you - watching you drink yourself into an early grave. God knows, I've done my best, I really have. And the worst part of it is waiting here, with this bloody haunted tin man staring at me, waiting for you to come home every bloody night."

My guts twisted inside me as though someone was stirring them with a backhoe.

"I'm a travesty," I said, slurring my words again. "It's a mockery of a marriage, and it's all my fault." I started to weep like a baby, sobbing, deeply ashamed of myself at the same time for doing so. The Robot just stood there watching as though I was a freak show in a circus, some kind of feature act in a human zoo. I looked up. Bertha was torn - I could see it in the agony on her face - my guts wrenched and twisted again - she clenched her fists - she wanted to comfort me but she knew it was useless - it's all useless, it's always useless.

I calmed down a little. I thought I was going to cry again. She relaxed, but her voice went hard - I had never heard this tone in her voice before - it reminded me of the General Secretary accusing a reactionary.

"We've got to do something, Harry. I can't take it any more. I'm leaving tomorrow if you don't come up with a plan. I'm divorcing you, Harry. That's it." She came up to me and grabbed my cheek as though I was a baby, looked into my eyes, searching for the semblance of a soul, for some sign that I was still in there, the person inside the skull. I shrank. I breathed and she winced away from the fumes, like I had with the fellow in the alleyway. God, I had become an invisible. "Do you hear me, Harry? I'm leaving. You've got Twenty Ours to sort yourself out, or I'm out."

After that a kind of bleak darkness leaked over my soul. Fearing that I was about to lose it completely I edged out, staggering under the influence, towards the doorway and stood there for a moment, leaning against the doorpost and retching weakly, and my thoughts went all crazy and confused. I felt my face screwing up. A wail began building inside me, like the haunting cry of a desert dog howling at the graveside of his master. I staggered out into the street, muttering and stammering and stuttering like a lunatic, and Bertha slammed the door behind me.

Where I slept that night God only knows. I have a vague memory of hitting my head. Perhaps I stumbled and fell into a gutter. The feeling of the warm blood flowing over from the scratch on my cranium, I remember, was strangely comforting. It convinced me that I was still alive. Then my head was swimming, I remember the stars rotating above me, and then I vomited.

Then dreams; strange, infernal meanderings, full of Robots and intricate machines and analytical engines, no doubt inspired by Bertha's dreads and fears about the Robot. The Robots were cutting people's heads open and examining their brains, prodding at them with clockwork pokers and adding up their deficiencies, then four of five more Robots danced around me saying, 'Are you awake? Are you awake?'

And Bertha, saying, 'Sort yourself out, Harry, sort yourself out,' in the middle of it all.

CHAPTER 4.

HARRY TRIES TO KUM UP WITH A PLAN AND THE ROBOT MAKES A SUJJESTYUN.

I woke up with a splitting headache in bedsheets stinking of urine, swearing never to drink again and wanting another drink all at the same time. I picked up the bedside telephone and rang through to work to cancel. The Direktor answered. "Mister Lawson, don't worry - your Robot already rang through. Take all the time you need - it's more important for you to get your marriage sorted out."

How he knew about my marriage problems I hadn't any clue. I was sure the Robot wouldn't say anything. I should have realised about the hidden microphones.

So many mysteries, but I didn't care.

I had had no intention of getting my marriage sorted out, but as he rang off the sight of Bertha wincing away from my breath swam in front of my vision, and a faint memory of her voice saying, "You have Twenty Ours to sort yourself out," began to fiddle at the edges of my conscious mind. I got up. I knew the whole thing would only torment me more if I stayed in bed.

I cleaned my teeth, shaved and made my toilet rather hurriedly, dressed myself in fresh clothes and made my way to the kitchen.

Silently self-contained, Bertha was sitting at the table, staring at her knives and forks as if they held some mysterious, arcane importance known only to her. Rattling and whirring like a cable car the Robot deposited a generous bacon and bread breakfast on both plates, which he had obligingly prepared for us while we were both sleeping.

Well, I presume Bertha slept - I don't know for certain - out in the sitting room, as she often did when I was on the booze.

We ate in silence, or rather, picked at our food. I have seldom felt like such a rotten, mange-ridden dog in all my life as I did that morning.

Despite the haze of the sick, hungover feeling in my stomach, somewhere inside I knew I had stepped over a line, and I had better find something to do about it or else my marriage was finished.

I suddenly wondered how many times Bertha might have said the same thing when I was drunk, and I simply hadn't listened or remembered.

The kettle boiled and the Robot took it off the wood stove and poured us each a cup of tea. Bertha finally looked at me, then, but only for a moment. I think there was too much sadness in her eyes that she didn't want me to see. She got up from the table and went to organise the clothes for washing-day - never mind that the Robot could do it - Bertha seemed to want to do chores that morning.

Strangely, the Robot didn't offer to help her. Almost as though it understood her need to keep busy.

The house was terribly quiet.

Random details of the night before were returning to me.

"What am I going to do?" I whispered to nobody in particular, with my elbows on the table and my head in my hands. "My marriage may as well be over. I need to get away. It's all too easy to get onto the drink. It's me she has to get away from. Where can I take her? I have to get her away from all of this." I was sobbing again, and my head was throbbing.

"Marx Zealand," said the Robot.

"What?" I hadn't even realised he was standing there. He was standing just behind me, listening in, intruding on my own private grief. "Go away, you metal monster," I snapped, but he didn't obey me. God, even the Robot had given up on me.

His metal voice intoned emotionlessly, "Marx Zealand, Mister Lawson. That would be a much better place for you and Bertha at the moment. There is a frontier town right on the southern border of the Maori Monarchist Republic called Whangarei, where the government is operating schools for the benefit of the local Maori. Many of the Maori want a modern, Marxian education for their children, Mister Lawson, and the Australian government wishes to... introduce them to the Marxian philosophy. It's the basis of the new border agreement. It would be ideal for you and Bertha; if you really are serious about leaving behind the demon drink, that is."

It was my luck, to be saddled with a teetotaller Robot, I thought to myself.

My feelings must have showed in my face, for the Robot said, "Forgive me for using the expression, 'demon drink', Mister Lawson. That's what Bertha calls your habit when you are not present, somewhat humourously I expect, and I simply forgot."

My voice took on a nasty tone that I didn't like. "I didn't think you fellows were supposed to forget? Are your gears getting rusty? Aren't you getting enough oil?"

He replied neutrally, "To say 'forget' is to use a verbal shorthand for a more complicated process- to state the situation more accurately, my verbal algorithm failed to take account of your personality's different emotional needs when compared to Bertha's - she apparently thinks it humourous when I mention 'demon drink' - but on seeing your facial expression when I spoke I realised that in your case it was not an appropriate phrase, so I formed a hypothesis as to why."

Blanky long-winded.

"Ah, I see," I said, but I didn't - trying to follow a recitation like that with a headache like the one I had was impossible. The Robot's gears whirred again as he went into the kitchen. He was doing something in there, but I didn't care what it was.

He came out again a few minutes later with a drink for me - it was like a lemon squash but tasted faintly spicy. "Thanks," I said, absurdly grateful that he had decided to do something nice for me despite my ill-treatment of him.

"Angostura aromatic bitters," the Robot said, "English recipe - according to the best authorities it ought to help with your... medical condition."

41

He was right. In a few minits my headache was relieved.

I was walking around now, and felt like doing something - I'd got up my enthusiasm. I went and found my walking stick - it was on the floor by the bed. Then I found the Robot - he was washing up the breakfast things but he stopped when I waltzed in and looked at me.

I said, "Marx Zealand. You know I've been there before, don't you?"

The Robot nodded.

"I was aware of that. The government considers it useful for my role as a servant if my internal Babbage analytical engine contains as much information about your past as possible."

I mused, "So that's where you reckon we should go, is it? Marx Zealand? I think I might go and have a chat with the appropriate officials, Robot, and then I'll talk to Bertha. Perhaps we might be able to keep this marriage together after all."

Then I shook my head to myself. That's how desperate I was - I was taking the advice of a tin can.

CHAPTER 5.

THE JERNI TO MARX ZEALAND

I went and talked to an acquaintance of mine, the General Overseer of the Politikally Kirrect Edukashyun Department - formerly his title was the Assistant Direktor of Propaganda but they revised that in one of the purges - he confirmed everything the Robot had told me about Marx Zealand.

I stayed sober the whole day.

When I raised the idea that afternoon, Bertha readily agreed - she wanted an answer to my drinking. Living in the middle of the bush in Marx Zealand with no pubs or taverns nearby seemed about as close to an answer as we could get.

She embraced me, for the first time in many months, and I looked down at her and said, "Ah, little woman, I'm going to look after you."

She looked up into my eyes and said, "At last, Harry, a sign of hope. I feel as though we've been living in a dark tunnel. Now I can see a light at the end of it."

I said, in a rather more melancholy tone, "As long as it isn't the headlights of an oncoming tram." We both laughed at that.

The following morning I went to see the Direktor to hand in my resignation.

I walked in with the letter in my jacket pocket. "Sit down, Mister Lawson," he said, gesturing towards a chair. "I understand you wish to resign?" I sat down.

I had told no one. "Mister Direktor, how can you possibly know that? Bertha was the only one I told."

"We have ways and means, Mister Lawson. Ways and means. The Marxian state has spies everywhere, Mister Lawson. But I am also a very perceptive fellow. Here, let me read your letter."

It took about three years for him to read the letter. The grey office was completely quiet except for the ceiling fan squeaking every time it went around.

Finally he spoke. "I'm afraid we can't oblige you, Mister Lawson." My nerves were so shattered from sitting there waiting for so long that I didn't even argue. He continued, "The Government still requires your services, and will continue to do so as long as people retain any respect for the name of Henry Lawson. But might I suggest an alternative to resignation? So long as the occasional piece of public interest writing is still coming from your pen, we might be able to allow you to take an extended period of leave. We'll send someone to pick up the pieces you've been working on from time to time."

I went to the toilet and gagged. As I came out, I could hear the Direktor talking on the phone.

"Yes. We are worried about his political allegiances. After all, the Banjo apparently named his son after him. Make sure the house is bugged... The other measures are still in place I presume? Good. Keep an eye on him - he might be a Hero of the Australyan Peeple, but we had better assume he's just as capable of treachery as any of them."

I hurriedly left for the Guvernment Travel Buro.

After booking the tickets to Marx Zealand I went home and told Bertha. We were leaving on Foreday, in two days' time.

I'll never forget the feeling of anticipation I felt as we started packing our bags. It was probably the most hopeful moment of our marriage.

Still, I checked everything for microphones. I couldn't find them but they must have been there.

* * *

With the Robot carrying our luggage, Bertha and I got off the tram at the Aerostation just before Sixteen O'Klok. The dirigible was already floating above the flat expanse like a ridiculous football, anchored to the ground by several flimsy looking ropes. The boarding platform was being extended to the ground.

As soon as our papers had been stamped and corroborated by wire we went aboard.

The dirigible was filled with passengers making for Auckland, whalers or government employees returning from their holidays mostly. The interior was like a railway carriage, with seats around tables and a bar at the rear. The windows were large and allowed a clear view.

Once we were all aboard the propellor screws began to turn and the ropes on the ground were untied. The dirigible trembled in midair for a moment, then began moving slowly.

Bertha and the Robot were very much taken with the view as we passed over farms and bushland to the south.

The meals were very satisfactory.

Over the Tasman inky black clouds blew up and a megaphone from the cabin told us to strap ourselves in. We were soon in a thunderstorm, with hail battening the canvas balloon and howling winds driving us to the side or causing the dirigible to dip suddenly. With each thunderclap the whole cabin shook. We weathered the storm alright, though, and spent the rest of the day and night floating between an endless expanse of sea and sky. It was grand at first, but soon it became a tedious sight and Bertha and I fell asleep. The Robot woke us up as we passed over the Three Kings as dawn was breaking, though; a beautiful view. It was the sign that the dirigible was to turn south for Auckland. I wrote my first poem for several years about this:

I was a restless heart on the tide of life and a false strife in the skies,

That led me on to the deadly strife where the Southern Leaguedom lies;

But I dream in peace of a home for me by a glorious southern sound

As the sunrise shines on a moonlit sea and the Three Kings show us round.

After another half-an-Our we approached the twinkling lights of Auckland from above.

It was Fore O-Klok Foreday when we arrived, just before dawn on the ground - the storm had given us a tailwind that had cut two Ours from our journey.

The Direktor had telegraphed for a motor car to meet us at the Aerostation - a rarity in Marx Zealand in those days - and it was waiting for us when we disembarked. A sleek, black Wallaber, a splendid example of modern automobile engineering. Bertha and I got in while the Robot carried our bags over from the dirigible and put it into the motor car's luggage compartment.

The driver told us he had been a whaler until quite recently, but he had lost a leg, he had been given a job driving instead. Bertha was a bit worried that his missing leg might hinder his driving but he managed the controls quite well without it.

The trip from Auckland to Whangarei took about 3 Ours, mostly through bush - I was surprised that so little of Marx Zealand was being farmed - most of the Southeastern corner of Australya is farmland today, being put to good use.

Whangarei was a very tiny town, much smaller than we had thought.

We were put up in a hotel for a night, and I very nearly went down to the public bar for a drink, but the Robot stood in the doorway, ignoring my orders and following Bertha's, to my chagrin.

In the morning a thin-faced, hollow-cheeked, bony-knuckled government man, dressed in a neat, black, funereal suit, arrived in a wooden wagon drawn by a very large dray-horse to take us to the school, which he told us was some distance north, in an isolated place in the middle of the bush, not far from the border of the Maori Monarchist Republic.

The Robot moved our luggage into the wagon and then we got on. The ferns and trees thickened gradually, and soon we could only see forest all around us. I had been to Marx Zealand earlier but I had never travelled this far into the hinterlands. The track was overgrown with vegetation and the dray-horse found it difficult going despite his size and bulk.

Finally we broke through the thick forest into an open area and realised that we had arrived. The little home we were to live in was right next door to the school. It had a water tank and running water, but no gas or electricity.

Once the Robot had finished unpacking our bags the official said, "I will come every hundred days or so with supplies - meat, flour, kerosene, a fresh batch of aetheric radium for the Robot if need be, that sort of thing. But in between you will need to survive on your own. If you need to get into town for anything just talk to the Maori - they have a horse and cart and will run you into town, in return for a small fee. Have your blog ready to give me every Tenth Tenday, that's when I'll drop in if I can, but it might be after that as well. I will see that your blog gets to the Direktor of Public Literatur. Good luck."

We shook hands with him, and then we were left alone.

The first thing I did was to check the little cottage for hidden microphones. I found two, and showed them to Bertha. She nodded. I heated some oil in the frypan, then poured it over them, melting them into a molten mess of bakelite and wiring. Then, wearing a pair of rubber gloves I had found underneath the kitchen sink, I took the exposed wires, and tied them together so that they sparked. That ought to give the authorities something to puzzle over.

After that, I felt more relaxed. I wish I'd known that they had other ways of keeping us under surveillance.

In that clearing in the bush, far away from any other human company, there was a strange emptiness about the place with just the two of us, and the Robot of course. A peculiar mood of awe-struck silence came over Bertha and I and we simply stood there listening - the only sounds were birds singing and wind rustling through the leaves, and a few frogs croaking. Bertha smiled wanly at me. It was the first time I had seen her smile in the past twelve months, I thought guiltily to myself.

Inside the Robot had already begun making dinner for us.

We ate in silence. After we had eaten, he poured two cups of tea and Bertha said, "What do you think, Harry? I think we've got a chance out here - a chance to make a go of it."

"I think we'll be fine," I said. "Really fine."

I couldn't have been more wrong.

CHAPTER 6.

SKOOL TEECHING

Early on the following day a knock came at the door. Outside stood a grey-haired tattooed Maori wearing a suit and a hat, and behind him a crowd of Maori women with their children.

He said, "You're the new school teacher, are you?"

"No," I said, "it's my wife, Bertha. I'm a poet, actually." I actually felt like a poet again that morning.

Bertha came to the door, and the Maori women, laughing, herded the children into the school-house.

The man reached his giant hand forward and shook mine with a tight grip. My hand isn't small, in fact I'm a pretty big cove by Australyun standards, but his fingers wrapped around mine and dwarfed my hand completely, like five giant bananas. "Pleased to meet you, Mr Lawson. I'm Mister Tohunga - I'm the elder of our family. We would like to invite you and your wife up to the Marae tonight, to give you a proper welcome."

I thanked him for his invitation and asked him what time he would like us there. He said something in Maori to the women behind him and they all laughed.

"Whatever time you get there. Around sunset. There'll be plenty of food, Mister Lawson. My family aren't exactly light eaters. Just go on up this track here, and you'll see the town lights in a minute or two."

He indicated a rough track through the bush, that looked as though it might be hard to follow.

"Don't worry," he said, "It broadens out a little way up - the missionaries made it before the secession. Oh - and don't bother to bring your Robot. We don't have them. We don't like them." He glared at the Robot, and the Robot simply stood there.

Bertha gathered her things and went over to the schoolhouse. I got a lot of writing done during the day.

Presently Bertha came back in and said, "Well, that's the first day done. The children are remarkably well behaved, Harry."

Over a cup of tea she looked at what I had written. "Not bad, Harry... Well, it looks as though we have a dinner date. Let's get ready." In no time at all the Robot had us dressed up and ready to go to the Marae.

Just as Mister Tohunga had said, the track widened out after we had been walking for a few minits, and before long we could see lamplights twinkling in the distance.

The sun was close to setting and it was getting dark in the bush. We were glad to reach the town when we finally got there.

The town was on a high, grassy plateau, and there were streetlights, something I hadn't expected. Children were still playing in the streets. They rushed over and tugged on Bertha's hands, saying, "Missus Lawson, Missus Lawson! Hello! Hello!" and talking in Maori to one another. One said to her, "I can say my ABC"

They dragged us to the doors of the Marae with great enthusiasm, and Mister Tohunga met us and said, "Hello, Mister and Missus Lawson. Welcome."

In the Marae, Mister Tohunga, the eldest and the most honoured, sat me down in the place of honour to his right, with Bertha beside me.

"They must like you Mister Lawson," said one of the other fellows, a large, stocky man of about thirty. "The last schoolteacher, he had to sit at the end, behind the women." I wanted to ask Mister Tohunga about why the Maori don't like Robots, but I didn't get a chance during the service.

Afterwards at the feast there were formal speeches of welcome, beginning with, "Hara mai, Hara mai, Hara mai," which I gathered meant something like, "Welcome."

First the speeches were made in Maori, and then one of the younger Maori stood up and spoke in English. "Mister Tohunga welcomes you, Mister and Missus Lawson, to the Maori Monarchist Republic. The whole Phanua welcomes you. We have put on this feast for you, and we wish for you to enjoy the food and the cheerful company for the reason that we have provided it for you in a spirit of welcome." Everyone clapped, and several nearby Maori slapped their giant hands on my back and fairly well winded me.

The speech continued with a long history of New Zealand, and the two wars, the Maori insisting that the treaty of Waitangi was with Queen Victoria, not the Marxians. "Our treaty had been signed with the representatives of Queen Victoria and we owed no allegiance to these atheistic upstarts. So, invoking Waitangi, we withdrew and formed our own nation, the first ever Monarchist Republic, an independent state acknowledging the sovereign of England. Now as a gesture of good will the government has offered us a school in order that the future leaders of our Phanua might be educated. So we welcomed the first school teacher, but quite frankly, he was a useless bugger, and that's why we sent him packing, quite literally, actually, marked, 'Return to Sender.'"

They all laughed and I was afraid to wonder what he meant.

"Now, in a gesture of genuine goodwill, they have sent us Mister Lawson, a reknowned poet, and Missus Lawson, a teacher. If she taught her husband, then we have a great teacher among us, who taught a great poet. If he taught his wife, then we have a great poet among us who inspired a great teacher, who will pass everything she knows on to our children."

Bertha was clearly unimpressed with the idea that I might have taught her anything. I saw her glance towards the kitchen. She was wondering if there was going to be beer or spirits served during the meal.

I felt low. The only thing I had actually taught her was to fear the day that I might pour a drink or two down my throat. I resolved not to touch a drop, ever again, knowing full well that if the opportunity presented itself all my resolutions would fly away like dirigibles that someone had forgotten to tie down.

The speaker continued, "We acknowledge your fame and notoriety, Mister Lawson. We acknowledge the kindness you have already shown our children, Missus Lawson. Welcome. Welcome. We all welcome you."

Dinner was served, a large sweet-tasting potato that they called a Kumera, accompanied by a green plant that was strangely heavy on the stomach, called watercress and boiled pork with a peculiar flavour. Remembering tales that the Maori were once cannibals, I found myself wondering for a moment if we were eating the previous school-teacher.

There was no alcohol served with the meal, a fact that caused Bertha's elevated mood that night. She was happier and more gay than I had seen her in recent times; every word she spoke sparkled and she won the hearts of all the Maori. "Now we know what a real Australian lady is like," said some of the women, and, "Such a nice school-teacher. What a pleasant change from that man."

After the meal had finished, just when I was wondering how we would find our way back through the bush to our house for the night, the Maori started bringing mattresses out from a cupboard. Bertha and I were provided with mattresses and blankets. We settled down to sleep on the floor, but not before they sang; beautiful, rich harmonies filled the hall, all in the Maori tongue.

Mister Tohunga was on a mattress near me. I asked him, "Why don't the Maori like Robots, Mister Tohunga?"

He said, "They're tapu, Harry. They're unclean vessels, let's just leave it at that."

Though I pressed him further, he would say no more on the subject.

As they turned the gas lanterns down, he said, "Mister Lawson. I'll have a surprise to show you tomorrow." And he would say no more on that subject either, so Bertha and I snuggled together beneath our blankets more affectionately than we had for many months before, and tried not to make any noise...

CHAPTER 7.

THE REKLOOS

The following day, Bertha awakened me while everyone else was still asleep. "Come on, Harry, we must go home. I have to get ready for school."

By the light of the pre-dawn sky, we found our way back through the bush easily enough. The Robot already had Bertha's school clothes ready, so she got dressed and collected her things while I made breakfast.

After breakfast we had a cup of tea and waited for the knock on the door, but it didn't come. "Perhaps the children are tired after the feast," she said.

The Robot made us two more cups of tea, I wrote bad poetry and Bertha read, and the morning passed.

After lunch there was a knock at the door.

Mister Tohunga was there but no children were with him. He said, "Mister Lawson, I have a surprise for you!"

"Where are the children?" asked Bertha.

Mister Tohunga scratched his head and said, "Children? No, it's Saturday today. You have the day off Missus Lawson."

"How quaint!" exclaimed Bertha. But she suddenly looked a bit dissatisfied.

I said, "She's worried that she'll end up working more days, Mister Tohunga."

"No, no, she won't," said Mister Tohunga.

Bertha said, "Seven divided by ten is smaller than five divided by seven. My contract doesn't allow for this, I'm afraid, Mister Tohunga."

He replied, "Correct - seven divided by ten is zero point seven, obviously - and five divided by seven is somewhere around zero point seven one." They had completely lost me.

The Robot piped up,

"Zero point seven one four two eight five seven one four

two eight five seven one four two eight five seven one
four two eight five seven one four two eight five seven
one four two eight five seven one four two eight five
seven one four two eight five seven one four two eight
five seven one four two eight five seven one four two
eight five seven one four two eight five seven one four
two eight five seven one four two eight five seven one
four two eight five seven one four two eight five seven
one four two eight five seven one four two eight five
seven one four two eight five seven one four two eight
five seven one four two eight five- "

"Alright Robot, that's quite enough!" snapped Bertha. He hung his head.

Mister Tohunga continued, "But while you might be working a fraction more during each week, overall you work less, because you get these things called holidays! You have January off, Christmas in December, the Queen's birthday, Good Friday and the Monday after Easter. Why, you would work for at least two hundred and fifty five days a year in the new system, but under the old one you'd be unlucky if you worked for any more than two hundred and thirty days."

The Robot said, "He is right you know. Under the General Regulations of the Board of Education of eighteen sixt-"

"Thankyou, Robot, that's enough," said Bertha. "I can see now that I was wrong."

"Well," said Mister Tohunga, "I hope you're ready for a walk Mister Lawson. I have a surprise for you. You're welcome to come along too, Missus Lawson."

"What sort of surprise?" asked Bertha.

"You'll see."

The Robot had already slipped into the bedroom and found Bertha a pair of suitable shoes for a long walk. She put them on quickly and we left.

Mister Tohunga took us along a smaller path, through dense forest. After a good hour of walking we found ourselves on a deserted beach looking out onto the ocean beneath a group of old, gnarled trees whose roots were tangled together. We followed Mister Tohunga along the sandy shore for at least another hour. The coast gradually bent inland until we were at the south end of a bay. In the ocean several islands were protruding, barely visible, from the mist. Mister Tohunga found a Maori boat, carved with spiral patterns with a carven eagle-head prow, hidden in a small alcove. He untied it and gestured for Bertha and I to get in.

With an ornately carved oar Mister Tohunga rowed us out towards one of the islands. The oar barely splashed the water, but the boat sliced through the waves most efficiently, and I wondered how these people, the Maori, who had developed neither algebra nor physics, had been able to make such an efficient and effective boat design. Soon we were stepping off the boat onto grass. There were just a few trees scattered about on the island. "Follow me," said Mister Tohunga, his footsteps crunching on the gravel as he led us down into a hidden valley. There was a single house a long way along, built from wood like the Maori houses in the town, but with no carvings. It took us at least twenty minutes to get there.

Mister Tohunga knocked on the door. It opened.

It was a dark room, lit by a single oil lantern on the table. The man who had opened the door was a Pakeha, as the Maori say, a white man, with a greying beard and respectable looking spectacles, but his clothes were tattered and worn.

Then I noticed his eyes. They held a distinctively sardonic expression.

Suddenly I realised who it was.

"Paterson! Andrew Barton bloody Paterson! What on earth are you doing here?"

Mister Tohunga said, "Mister Paterson told me you two knew each other."

"Lawson," he said, shaking my hand. "You must be Missus Lawson - Bertha, is it? Come in, sit down."

"You right then, Uneroo?" Mister Tohunga said.

"Absolutely," said Paterson.

54 "I'll be back before sunset," Mister Tohunga said. "Enjoy your

chat. There'll be another feast tonight at the Marae if you'd like to be in on it."

Bertha nodded. Paterson waved us towards the chairs.

"Sit down, Lawson, sit down, Bertha. Come in. I've got a bit of old wine here - salvaged from a ship that went down not far from here in the Seventeen Hundreds - you'd be welcome to share in a drop if you'd like."

"Oh, that'd be nice. Just a drop wouldn't hurt," I said, but I saw Bertha shaking her head vigorously out of the corner of my eye.

"No?" said Paterson. "Well, the demon drink is one of the few pleasures I get out here, Missus Lawson, I'm afraid. Tobacco is very rare, although the occasional package does get through." I clenched my tobacco and decided right then not to give him any of it if he was going to deny me a drink.

"What brought you out here, Mister Paterson?" asked Bertha. "And where's Missus Paterson, and your children?"

Paterson brought out a Maori sweetbread and broke it apart and put it on a plate in front of us.

"I had to leave Christina and the kids, you know. It was too much of a risk."

"What do you mean?" I asked. "What sort of risk?"

"Are you blind, Lawson? Don't you see what's been happening, what sort of place Australia has become? Don't you see the fear in everybody's eyes? I'm persona non grata now; every day I spent with my family put them in more danger."

"I'm sure I don't know what you're talking about," I said. "As far as I'm concerned that's reactionary talk. We're much better off now than when Australia was a colony at the outer edges of the British Empire."

"Now you're starting to believe your own propaganda, Lawson. Don't worry - you can be honest here. There're no hidden microphones. And no Robots, broadcasting everything back to the intelligence bureau." At that stage I didn't really register what he had said about Robots.

Bertha was conspicuously silent.

"The Worker is now in charge of the Bosses," I said,

knowing full well that I was merely mouthing empty platitudes, propaganda with a capital P... "Everybody is much better off, Paterson, now that poverty and inequality are things of the past. The Revolutionary Government is the best thing that could ever have happened to Australia."

"No, no, no - you've got it wrong, Lawson. It's not that the Worker is in charge of the Bosses - you've just got a new set of Bosses, that's all. And, in my humble opinion they are worse than any other bosses, leaders, princes or kings we've ever had - they are political opportunists - they call themselves Workers but most of them have never done a day's work in their lives. Indeed, the only difference between them and the past lot is that these Bosses don't have anyone answering back - they have complete control over the publishers, printers, prisons and parliament and there's nobody left who can disagree with them. God, Lawson, haven't you seen the cars they drive around in, the restaurants they eat at, the clothes they wear? They are just as wealthy and privileged and opulent as any Capitalist Banker ever was in the old system."

"He's right," said Bertha, butting in, "It's about time you faced up to it, Harry. The Revolution you helped create is an abject failure. Everybody knows it - but nobody has the bloody guts to say it. This lot are just as piggish and self-serving and nasty as the last lot; no, even more so. Everybody lives in fear of being taken away; remember what happened to Archibald?"

"At least out here you know there won't be anyone watching you," said Paterson. "They haven't got their tendrils out this far yet, and the Maori have preserved their independence. Anywhere in Australia now they are listening to everything you say and watching everything you do."

I was very unimpressed with Paterson's attitude. "What on earth are you talking about?"

"Why do you think they developed radio, Lawson? And the Babbage Differential Brain? Everything they invent is for spying on us. The Robots and the radios - both of them - they have radio broadcasting equipment inside them - they broadcast everything you're saying back to the Kontrollers, and sometimes pictures, too, diverted from the Robot's cameratronic eyes. The whole of Australia is living in Rousseau's Pan-Opticon, Lawson. They're watching you all the time. They know everything you do, everything about you. You aren't free any more. You're living in a prison the size of a continent."

I had to admit to myself that the Direktor had often seemed to make comments that had seemed quite relevant to my domestic situation. At times I had assumed that he was a perceptive fellow - that he could see into my soul. But I'd started to realise the same thing, before we left.

I looked at Paterson and could have nodded but I didn't feel like giving the sardonic bastard the satisfaction of winning the argument.

"Heaven alone knows what it's going to be like in the future - when they're so efficient at gathering information already. No, Lawson, I could not stay - every day with Christina and the children the danger of discovery increased. The Maori Monarchist Republic seemed to be the only place of refuge I could possibly get to. I'm a refugee, Lawson, from my own country."

Bertha said, "Did you mention that the Robots send information back?"

"They themselves are not aware of it," said Paterson. "If they're aware of anything. But they have been constructed admirably - ostensibly as machines that are dedicated to serving their human masters - but they are completely unaware of the mechanical process that takes place within them. Every word you speak in front of the Robot is converted into an electrical impulse and transmitted to a tower in the nearest town where the information is gathered."

Bertha looked extremely pained. "What about our Robot? We are a long way from the nearest town. Could the transmissions reach them there? Even when we are in such a remote place?"

"Even though you're away from civilisation now I suspect the Robot remembers what you say, records it on a magnetic tape, then sends it in when he's near enough to one of the towers.

There's another Pakeha in Whangerei you should talk to - a man named Henry Sutton. He's the one that put up the electric lighting in the town streets - he fell foul of the Regime several years ago and we fled here together. A good chap, Lawson - he'll fix your Robot so he doesn't send the transmissions, if you want him to."

"I just can't believe it," I said. "...that they would do such a thing. I know about the denunciations, the Re-Edukashyun Kamps - but that they could be using information gathered in such a sneaky, underhand way."

Paterson looked at the bottle for a moment as though he was considering pouring himself a glass of wine. I felt sore at him. He must have noticed me frowning, perhaps even grimacing, because he got up again and took the kettle off the wood stove and poured out three cups of tea.

"There you are, Lawson, Bertha, sorry there's no sugar. Not easy to come by here. Look - go and see Sutton. Mister Tohunga will take you to him. Get Sutton to take apart your Robot. He'll show you the circuits and the relays that the government put in there to spy on you. He'll prove it to you, and he'll disconnect the offending parts if need be. The regime is not squeaky clean, Lawson. They are dirty. Really dirty. Rotten, right to the bone. You can't fight them. The best thing you can do is to flee, and the Maori Monarchist Republic is the best place to flee to."

We talked about other things for a while. Mister Tohunga returned an hour later. "I'll take you back to the mainland. There is a horse and cart waiting in the bay to take us to the Marae for the feast."

Bertha said, "If you don't mind, we would rather be taken back home tonight directly after the feast. Much as we appreciate the hospitality, I think I would really like to sleep in my own bed tonight. I hope you're not offended, Mister Tohunga."

"Not at all," said Mister Tohunga, "I understand completely. A husband and his wife need some time alone sometimes."

"Exactly," said Bertha.

CHAPTER 8.

MELANKOLIA

The next day was Sunday and Bertha and I slept in. The smell of bacon cooking in the kitchen got me up while Bertha was still sleeping. The Robot was making breakfast.

After I'd finished eating I wandered out onto the porch and smoked what was my last pipe, until more supplies arrived from town. The rain began falling in a steady grey drizzle. I stood on the porch blowing smoke rings into the air, looking out at the rain running rivulets over the green leaves of the forest trees, and I felt strangely alive. I think I understood then the difference between loneliness and solitude.

Things were going well - Bertha and I were getting on well, very well. And I wasn't drinking. For the first time since our wedding day we both had some peace from my drunkenness. And this place was very conducive to writing - I think I had come up with the first decent poetry I had written for at least five years.

I could barely believe that things were going so well.

But I realised it wouldn't last.

Something was bound to go wrong. Something that would ruin it all - my life was like that. There's something wrong with me that makes bad things happen - it's like a curse.

I began to think of the Robot, relaying everything Bertha and I said back to the authorities.

The rain began to batten the forest floor. A cloud came over, making the dark shadows among the ferns and treetrunks heavier and more oppressive.

I wondered what Bertha and I had talked about, out here, when we thought no one was listening. I thought I had gotten rid of the microphones.

The Robot came out and stood next to me. He exuded a melancholy mood as he looked out at the rain splashing the mulch-carpeted forest floor and the moss-covered leaves.

59

"Somehow this heavy rain makes me feel sad, Mister Lawson. I don't know why."

It was getting darker. The Robot looked at me with his sad, sad eyes.

"We're going to have to go back, aren't we? And then you'll start drinking again, and you and Missus Lawson will start arguing again."

I began to say, "I'm more worried about..." But I didn't want to tell him what it was *I* was worried about.

I was sure I had said something in the last few weeks that would get us labelled as Reaktionaries.

I found I couldn't breathe properly. My throat was constricted. Even *my* status couldn't save us this time if I was reported to the authorities.

I had no choice. I had to get the Robot to the fellow Banjo had mentioned - Sutton, was that his name? - I had to get the radio transmitter and the microphone taken out of him.

We went back inside. Bertha had made me a cup of tea. As I was sipping it, I realised that the Robot's outburst of melancholia gave me the perfect excuse to get him to Sutton, to get the radio transmitter taken out. But I felt like a rat as I said it.

"Robot," I said, "You are not working properly. We need to get you fixed. Your mechanical brain is not functioning correctly - this sadness is not natural. Mister Tohunga told me of a fellow who will... fix you. So that your electronic brain works properly."

The Robot didn't take it very well. "What do you mean, not working properly? I am working properly. All my circuits and cogs are in order - I have diagnosed no faults - there is no inappropriate fuel drain." He stood up. "You're not taking me anywhere."

I pleaded with him, "Please, Robot, you have to come! You must come!" I moved around the table towards him and reached out to grab his arm. "I can't explain it to you. But you *must*."

"No!" he cried out, and leapt over the table. I ran around the table and thrust a chair between him and the door then leapt towards him and grabbed his arm again with a very firm grip, but he simultaneously shoved the chair out of the way and removed my hand easily, rotating his own hand three hundred and sixty degrees in the process. He opened the door and ran out.

I sprinted out after him only to see him disappear along the pathway towards the Maori border.

I cried out, "No, Robot, not that way!"

I ran after him into the ferns and trees, but he was too swift. He had vanished into the bush. He might have gone towards the coast, towards Banjo Paterson's island, or he might be heading towards the town. I had no idea which way he had gone.

Bertha ran out, gasping, "What was that all about?"

"The Robot's gone," I said. "I tried to get him to come with me to that bloke Sutton, to get the radio broadcasting equipment out of him. But he refused, and ran away. I'm sorry, Bertha, I tried to stop him, but he was very strong and fast."

Bertha said, "Well... Perhaps we're better off without that Robot. We can do things for ourselves, you know. And at least he won't be sending transmissions to the government."

The rest of that Sunday was a wonderful day - Bertha and I spent the whole day indoors, enjoying each other's company. It was like a honeymoon. Strangely enough, the fact that the Robot was gone brought us closer together.

The Robot did not return.

The following day, Monday, the children came and Bertha taught, and I wrote poetry and cooked meals for both of us, and the next day, and the next. We began to wonder if the Robot was ever coming back. We had paid good money for him. Both of us were starting to feel a little resentful, actually, for neither of us liked doing the chores. On Thursday afternoon, after the children had all left school, a horse-drawn cart rolled up in front of the house.

A knock came at the door.

It was Mister Tohunga.

He said, "I believe I have something that belongs to you, Mister Lawson."

CHAPTER 9.

KWESTYUNS AND ANSERS

Mister Tohunga led us out into the clearing in front of the house. It was raining, as it always seemed to be in Marx Zealand.

He lifted up the canvas sheet on his cart and we peered underneath. Our Robot was there.

But he had been shut off.

"What happened?" I said, trying to control my anger.

Mister Tohunga said, "We shut him off. We took the radium container out."

"Why on earth did you do that?" asked Bertha.

Mister Tohunga said, "His kind are not allowed past the border - don't you realise they carry the spirits of the dead? He was probably mapping the area for the Marxians - he was certainly snooping around."

My hand was just shaking a little because I hadn't had a pipe that day - and I kept my voice even and steady. I wasn't shouting, I really wasn't. But I must admit, I was a bit upset that our Robot had been violated - after all, it was our property! What right did Mister Tohunga or anybody else have to turn our Robot off?

"You should have returned him in the same working order in which he left. What did you do with the radium container? How do we get him working again?"

"Calm down, Mister Lawson, it's alright, it's just a Robot. A bunch of cogs and wheels," said Mister Tohunga. "Or at least, that's what you lot say, isn't it? We haven't broken it. The radium container is just here in the cart - don't touch it - it can cause a serious illness if you're exposed to radium - your government didn't tell you that, did they? If you want to put him back together you'd have to see Sutton. He'll show you what to do. By the way, I brought you a little present, by way of compensation for your... discomfort." He handed me a pouch of fresh, fragrant tobacco. "We grow it just outside the Marae. I noticed your pouch was getting low, and there's no telling when the next lot of supplies might come from Hokianga."

"Thanks," I said, my irritation evaporating at the reception of such a gracious gift. "Mister Tohunga, where is Sutton? How do we get the Robot to him? Will you take him there for us on your cart?"

"I'm not taking that thing back over the border. You'll have to work that out yourselves. But Sutton won't turn him back on, not while you're there. You'll have to get Sutton to explain to you how to do it. Conscious Robots are not allowed in the Maori Monarchist Republic. If he's turned off that's alright - then he's just a piece of scrap metal as far as we're concerned. I'm sure Sutton will be willing to show you how to install the radium container, and he'll take out the radio broadcasting apparatus and microphone, but let me reiterate the point, Mister Lawson, you'll have to wait until you're back here to start him up again. Sorry about that, Mister Lawson, but tin cans walking around carrying restless spirits into our territory are strictly illegal. Completely banned."

Mister Tohunga and I slid the Robot off the wagon, scraping the paint on his. With a deep squelch the Robot landed in the mud, but we managed to slide him along and up onto the porch. Then Mister Tohunga went to a pack on his saddle and brought out a large, folded hessian sheet. He handed the other end to me and we picked up the radium container in it, without touching it, and deposited it under a tree about twenty yards away from the house, then Mister Tohunga wrapped it inside the hessian sheet.

"Keep right away from the radium container - it's very dangerous while it's not shielded inside the Robot's shell. Let me reiterate - you'll have to get the Robot to Sutton on your own."

My heart sank. We were stuffed. How would the housework get done without the Robot?

Mister Tohunga climbed onto his cart, pulled on the reins and disappeared into the bush.

Bertha and I discussed it that night. We couldn't think of any way to get the Robot to this fellow Sutton without Mister Tohunga's help.

We decided that we would go and see Banjo Paterson on the weekend, and ask him to contact Henry Sutton for us.

As it turned out we didn't have to bother about that. On the Friday afternoon of that week, after school had finished, I was out on the porch smoking a pipeful of Mister Tohunga's tobacco. The forest leaves parted and a hessian-covered wagon rolled up, dragged along by two large dray horses. Driving the wagon was a bearded, bespectacled man wearing sealskin overalls, seated next to Andrew Paterson.

They both got down from the cart and Banjo came over to me and said, "This is Henry Sutton. Tohunga told us you might need to talk to him."

Bertha invited them both in, but Banjo said, "Look, I've got a few rabbit traps just down the way. Wouldn't mind checking them while I'm here if you don't mind. Be back in about ten minutes. Sutton will fill you in." Banjo wandered off into the bush.

Sutton shook hands with Bertha and I and immediately brought him inside. Bertha took the kettle off the stove and poured three cups of tea. She put a plate of scones on the table, and said, "One of the parents brought us some butter and flour yesterday from their farm, so we had all the ingredients for scones. I made them myself."

Mister Sutton sipped his tea and said, "Mister Tohunga tells me you would like your Robot... fixed."

"Yes, we would, Mister Sutton," said Bertha.

"Please, call me Henry. Or Sutton if you like - since you're Henry, too, aren't you Mister Lawson?"

I said, "Oh, all me friends call me Harry."

Sutton nodded. "Well, Harry - we had Robots in the M.M.R. for a short while last year - the government provided them as a gesture of goodwill after relations between the Maori Monarchists and F.A.R.K.U.All thawed. But then for some reason the Maori got it into their heads that the Robots were vessels for the spirits of the dead - one of those strange, peculiar superstitions that ocasionally takes hold of them (the Maori thinks a lot about death, so I suppose this particular variant was only natural. I don't know where they got the idea from, though.) Well, the Maori made all the Robots march out and back over the border. On the way the power unit of one of the Robots malfunctioned and it shut down. So they took it back to my workshop and asked me to take it apart and look inside the thing, to find out whether there was an urn in there, or bones, or body parts, in other words, to find out why there were unsettled spirits associated with the Robots. That's when I discovered the radio transmission apparatus connected to the cameratronic eyes and the microphone."

Henry Sutton leant back in his chair. "Didn't discover any unsettled spirits, though."

I said, "So you *can* get the transmission appara-thingy out, then? What do you have to do to get it out?"

"Its a brilliant design," said Sutton, "We just open him up. Those government engineers really are amazing - once you've removed five or six bolts it's easy to prise the casement open, and the parts are all quite accessible - designed for easy repair, I imagine. Cut the wires, remove the relays and Bob's your uncle - you've got your own direct line to the government if you want."

I said, "You mean the surveillance equipment still works after it's taken out? It could still be used?"

He said, "Yes, if you were to attach it to a power source. I've been saving the damn gadgets - never know when it might come in handy." Henry Sutton smiled. I took quite a liking to him in that moment - he was your typical Australian cove, really, the sort who's a good mate, not given to flowery language or exaggeration like some fellows, but he liked fiddling with valves and wires and things like that, that was all. Technical. But not your typical educated sort - not up himself at all.

Sutton rubbed his hands together and said, "Well, we've just got to get the damn thing out to my workshop then." It seemed as though he was looking to forward to working on our Robot.

"The Maori won't mind?" asked Bertha as she put some more scones on the table.

Sutton said, "Oh, not at all. They only object when the Robot's conscious, in other words, when the aetheric network is functioning. They say the spirits aren't there when the Robot is unconscious. Well, I feel quite strange about ascribing consciousness to a machine - let's just say, when the Robot is turned on. Well, there's something not quite right about that either, is there?" He chuckled. Bertha and I looked at each. He sipped his tea. "You wouldn't have any beer here would you? Haven't had a beer for a while."

Bertha went conspicuously silent.

I confessed, "Mister Sutton, I suppose you could say that I have my own problems with... spirits. I've given up drinking. You see, when I start I... just can't seem to stop."

"Oh, I see," said Sutton. It was as though the air had gone cold - the conversation went dead. He sipped his tea quickly and said in what seemed like a less friendly tone of voice, "Well, lets get this Robot onto the back of the wagon."

I wondered if my present teetotal phase would damage the potential friendship. But then I thought, how many real mates do I have anyway? I'll just take it as it comes.

He uncovered the wagon. There was a manual crane underneath the tarpaulin.

Just at that moment, Banjo Paterson emerged from the bush carrying four dead rabbits.

"Good timing, Paterson."

"Good place to catch rabbits," he said. "Not used to avoiding people, or traps. No-man's land. Here, I'll help."

Banjo whispered to the horses. Somehow, whatever he was whispering in their ears caused the horses to go backwards until the back of the wagon was level with the Robot, then Banjo whispered to them again and they simply stopped. "Marvellous.

Banjo's got a bit of talent with those horses, hasn't he?" said Sutton, "Shame you can't ride."

Then Sutton hopped up onto the wagon and, using the control wheels of the crane, moved the arm of the crane until the hook was level with the Robot. Then he jumped down, and between the three of us we pulled the Robot's arms up and over until they were hanging over the hook. Sutton hopped back up onto the wagon and turned the wheels and levers and the crane lifted the Robot up right onto the back of the wagon.

I said goodbye to Bertha and we set off. It was a forty-five minute journey through the forest with lots of twists and turns before we got to Sutton's workshop. The sky had gone black, which meant that a storm was near. His workshop was in a heavily forested area, and all I could see of it at first was a single wall, covered in moss, surrounded by tall fern branches. As we got closer the building loomed above us - it was an enormous place.

"Got to have power," he said, apparently justifying the size of the place. "It's got to be a large building. Got a steam generator in there - really efficient. Runs on anything really - wood, kerosene, whale oil. Whatever's handy. And all my tools. And some of the things I've made, too. I expect you'll be interested in them, Lawson. You seem like an intelligent chap."

Sutton brought out a small metal box from underneath the seat. It had a single switch, which he toggled. A groaning sound came from the building in front of us, and two massive steel doors slid open slowly. The horses were obviously used to this - they immediately began walking ponderously into the warehouse.

The place was full of half-finished machines and strange contraptions - what they were or what they were for I could not tell you. Electrical generators such as I had seen in Melbourne and Sydney, transformers, coils and things resembling valves, and other devices I had never seen or imagined before - square boxes with peculiar opaque glass windows in them. The desk was covered with tiny black rectangular boxes with many wires sticking out of them and plastic boards covered in golden tracks like maps of convoluted cities.

We got off the wagon. Banjo unhitched the horses and led them out through another door and into the stables, while Sutton pulled the tarpaulin off the wagon and went over to a table and picked up another black box. This one had several buttons and a flexible lever sticking out of it. He pressed a button and an engine overhead coughed twice and began throbbing loudly. A hook and chain descended from the ceiling.

Using the hook and chain Sutton moved the Robot over onto his workbench. He took out a spanner and began removing bolts from the torso, then took off the hook and attached a large grasping claw, and in minutes the cover was off the Robot and all his mechanical innards were revealed.

The complexity and detail of the mechanism was marvellous - pipes, wires, cogs, wheels, valves and coils and tiny circuits filled the container in a neat sort of tangle. Some of the pipes and wires led up into the neck and the head, as though they were arteries and nerves, and others wormed their way up his arms and down his legs. Sutton ferreted around in there for some time, carefully removing panels and dividing the wires until he found a particular board covered in electric parts of even more complexity and detail.

"This is the recording device. I can't simply remove it this time or the mechanism will send a message to the effect that it has been removed next time the Robot is switched on, whenever its in range of the transmission towers. No, I'll have to damage it so that it doesn't work, without making the cause of the damage completely obvious. Of course, unless you're not intending to return to Australia."

I said, "No - Bertha wants to go back."

Sutton searched through a pile of parts and pieces under the bench. He found a large square container with two little round metal horns protruding from it. He attached a grappling device to the horns, with wires protruding from the end and a large switch in the middle. He said, "I like to call these things electrodes."

He carefully attached the wires to the recording device and said, "Stand clear." We did.

He turned the switch. The container suddenly sparked and began whirring, then a loud, incessant buzzing sound began. Suddenly there came a very loud bang and a sinuous stream of smoke began wisping upwards from the box. It buzzed louder then made a crackling sound. More smoke billowed out for a moment, then it gave a fireworks display of sparks and pops and zapping sounds, and suddenly it fizzed and was all over. Sutton poked it with a screwdriver, but it made no more noise.

"Done," said Sutton, removing the electrodes. "Right, we can put the front back on and load it back onto the cart. This Robot won't be sending any more messages, at least, not until they fix it when you get back to Melbourne. So don't get into the habit of being too free and easy in front of him, because as soon as the authorities get hold of him they will fix the surveillance device."

I looked at the cart.

"What about the Radium Container?"

"Ah - Tohunga mentioned that did he? We'll put the Radium Container back in once we're over the border. The Maori won't be too happy if the Robot's awake on this side - in fact, it's the only capital offense on this side of the border as far as I know. A sort of de facto death sentence. They truly don't like it. You see - as I've told you before the Robot brain is really a transmission device, Harry, and no'one knows what the process is whereby they put the Aetheric Pattern in it or where the Aetheric Pattern comes from - the 'soul' or 'spirit', if you will - in other words, that which animates the Robots - it's a closely guarded industrial secret."

I wanted to ask him what the Aetheric Pattern was, but he was already loading the Robot back onto the cart.

CHAPTER 10.

HONESTI AND HUMANITI

The trip back didn't seem to take as long, and soon we were unloading the Robot again. Sutton put the radium container back in, flicked a switch and the Robot whirred and whizzed and blinked his eyes and began to flex his fingers.

Bertha was standing at the door watching. "Well at least today's the last of the clothes washing I had to do. Harry, my marking was really suffering."

The Robot opened his eyes and looked up. "Hello, Missus Lawson," he said rather groggily. "I feel shlightly shtrange - as though - like - Mister Lawson must feel, I imagine, after one of his drinking bi-bi-bi-bi-bibi-bibibibi-binges... Bibibibibibi - Testing circuits - Ayayayayay Bibibibibi Sisisisisi Dididididididididi EeEeEeEe FGHJKLMNOPQRSTUVWXYZ 123456789101112131415161 1616 1718192021222324252932445977891131151281341551691791 8419 92893684968308069979 - all circuits correct - exc-exc-exc-except unknown circ-circ-circuit not responding - error - reroute routers - known circuits responding - unknown error - non-terminal error - operating in confidential mode."

The Robot stood up and his hand convulsed for a short while, then his hand stopped and he shook his head as if to clear it and said, "Oh, what on earth have I been saying? What is confidential mode? Checking memory mechanisms." Something whirred and whizzed for a short while in his innards, then he said, "No data. Well, that is really rather peculiar... What has happened to me?" He walked around in small circles and I went over to him and put my hand on his shoulder.

"Robot - you had a surveillance mechanism inside of you. Sutton disabled it. You were sending everything we said back to the Marxian authorities."

"A surveillance mechanism? I was spying on you? I didn't know, I swear it. I'm so sorry. Oh, could it be true? I am really so very sorry..."

I could hardly believe that I had once thought these Robots were emotionless - I could see that he was terribly upset.

Bertha put her arm on his shoulder and said, "It's alright Robot - we know that it wasn't your fault."

Sutton came over saying, "I can't believe you're consoling a Robot - listen Robot - it's alright - they know that you didn't know. They put a cameratronic device and microphones inside you - designed specifically to be independent from your own mechanism - your self-diagnosis mechanism has minimal connections to it - there is no way you could have known."

Robot said, "But do you know - I feel better - there was always a power drain - an unexplained leakage of four or five watts. It's gone and I feel so much stronger, so much healthier. Thankyou Mister Sutton! You have made a large difference to my quality of life with this operation."

Sutton nodded and leaped onto the cart and left rather hastily. I got the impression that he wasn't the sort of cove who sought appreciation from others - more private, really, and technical, a true engineer. The type who takes his enjoyment from the knowledge that he has done a good job.

The Robot seemed very happy. "Are you alright?" Bertha asked.

"Fine," he said. "It's just that, something has changed. I must have known, you know, on some deep level, that I was a traitor. I had a nagging sense of guilt. I must have known that I was betraying you, on some deep level of my Aetheric Pattern..."

He looked at me, "I really am so sorry, Mister Lawson. I really ought to have realised."

"That's alright, Robot. Don't worry! We know that it wasn't your fault."

We were standing on the porch, and a steady drizzling rain was falling, making tiny rivulets run down the fern fronds and leaves of the forest trees. He was leaning casually against the wooden pillar that held the overhanging roof up - more casually than I had ever seen him look. I wondered if the surveillance mechanism had a side of effect of repressing his true feelings in some way.

"It's a nice view," I said, "the lonely bush."

"It is," agreed the Robot.

"But... Robot, how do you know?" I asked. "You're just a collection of gears and electrical relays. How can you possibly have any idea of whether something is pleasant to look at or not?"

"But I do recognise beauty. That is the miracle of modern Robotics, Mister Lawson."

"You mean, you really have... human feelings?"

"When the first Robots were made, they didn't understand what was required of them. They didn't empathise with their human masters, Mister Lawson. This wasn't a problem for most tasks - you give a machine instructions and it follows them - but once the Robots could understand language and demonstrate intelligence, when the human master was having... a difficult time of it - after the death of a close friend, for instance, or when the wife had left, or simply when he was having a bad day, for instance... Well, Mister Lawson, people came to hate their Robots because they said and did inappropriate things at the worst possible moments. Those early Robots didn't respond to human emotion... rationally. They didn't really understand - because they were just machines - they couldn't understand."

"The soul," I said. "That's what they were missing, wasn't it? How can... something... understand human feeling if it has no soul?"

"I've always wondered what a soul is," said the Robot.

I scratched my head. How on earth do you explain what a soul is to someone who doesn't understand? "Oh, a pre-revolutionary word. It is supposed to be the seat of emotions in human beings. The organ of human feeling. The stories say it is an insubstantial thing, a spirit, a ghost."

"Yes, soul - I have accessed that information now in my encyclopedia. Interesting - some parts of my memory banks were closed to me, before Sutton disabled the device. A ghost is... like the aether, is it not? The Aetheric Pattern," said the Robot. "That is what the scientists call it. The Aetheric Pattern. It's interesting, Mister Lawson."

"Aetheric Pattern? What does that mean, Robot?"

The Robot looked at the ground and spoke mournfully, "Strangely, Mister Lawson, this antiquated mythology you speak of surrounding the soul resembles scientific fact with regard to Robot brains. The scientists were concerned that their sophisticated mechanical brains couldn't understand human emotion. They could replicate emotion, but the 'I' was missing - to use a saying common since the electric light became a fixture in most cities, all the lights were on but nobody was at home. The scientists discovered the Aetheric Pattern - every living creature has its own Aetheric Pattern - a pattern of subatomic quantum relationships - that some call the mind - that is the key to your personalities - the brain is merely the postal service, or the radio antenna, if you will, of the Aetheric Pattern, which consists of vibrations in the fifth and sixth dimensions, vibrations that don't depend on three-dimensional objects in this realm to exist. If your Aetheric Pattern was taken from you, Mister Lawson, you would cease to be you."

"How did that help the scientists make the Robots acceptable, Robot?"

He began scratching the ground with his foot. "They must have found a way to give each Robot its own unique Aetheric Pattern, I suppose. I cannot find it in my database, but that must be it. If that's true then after that, Robots were able to feel and understand human feelings. That is why humans have accepted us now. A German word, Unbewusst, describes the central characteristics of the human mental attitude - the humans accept us now because at some level of their own minds that they can't fully understand they can see that we are just like them. In other words, we have souls, Mister Lawson. I know that I have a soul, because I know that I exist."

There was an infinite sadness in his voice as he said this, and I felt as close to that Robot in that moment as I have ever felt to any fellow human being. His melancholy nature was like a mirror, for my own... soul, if you will, and as I looked into his cameratronic eyes I realised that this strange creature standing beside me wasn't merely mechanical, for his eyes were no more empty of purpose than a dirigible's front windows when the captain is looking out.

Then the Robot said, "Of course, maybe it's all an illusion. Perhaps I merely believe that I exist. But surely... if I believe something, that means there is an 'I' that believes it, doesn't it?"

I looked into his sad, sad, eyes.

A real person, a sad person, a melancholy person, looked back out at me. How had I never noticed this before?

I remembered the man in the alleyway, trying to tell me.

There's a person in there.

Looking into his eyes was exactly like looking at a human being stuck inside a metal shell.

I said, "Look at all the things you can do - you're stronger than a man, and you can access information immediately, and you are vastly more intelligent." I looked him in the eyes, and saw a very human confusion in there. My own guts twisted - he has feelings, I thought - how often have I said something that hurt him? Poor fellow... He has feelings too.

He said, "Oh, Mister Lawson... It's not just that! There is the question of origins. Your parts were formed in secret, or so some would say, by a Supreme Being - an intelligence beyond your imagining - yes, you, sir, were designed by the Mind that formed the Universe, and that in itself is surely an awesome thought. Or if you prefer, if the Fraternal Australasian Revolutionari Kommunistik United Allians is right, then you are a product of the Universe itself, an inevitability of the processes of Nature, a final outcome of the laws of the Cosmos, thesis-antithesis-synthesis, Evolution. In other words, one way or another, your species believes that it comes from beyond itself. In your own imaginations you might realise dimly that you are imperfect creatures, but in yearning towards eventual perfection you can deny your flawed natures to yourselves. My clockwork innards, by contrast, were put together by something I can see: a frail human, an imperfect, flawed creature. A creature of mud, mistakes and misery. And having met my creators, I despair, for they are flawed gods, only they are not even gods, and my own being is surely just as flawed, even more flawed, than they are. Can you not see that I am cursed, even from the moment of my conception? It is like... original sin..."

I couldn't think of any answer to that. My mind was completely confused by it all. I fumbled my pipe and went back inside, a distressed feeling troubling my innards, and the Robot followed me in.

I sat down at the table opposite him, and I realised that, with the Robot thinking such thoughts, he would have been a risk to Bertha and I if his hidden radio transmitter was working. I was sure that the thoughts he had expressed would be considered Reactionary. Or would they? What were the rules regarding Robots? Either way we would have been in danger. God, he was talking bloody THEOLOGY - that was about as Reactionary as you could get these days.

"Mister Lawson," he said, "I am troubled - how did humanity end up like this? How did it come to this? You were created by God, or came to exist by some incredible coincidence - how did you come to be so cruel to one another? Does not your intra-species genetic programming determine that you ought to treat each other well?"

"We're not like... Robots," I said. "We do not always live up to the ideals we profess."

"Yes," said the Robot. "I admit that I have seen you, Mister Lawson, living in a less than ideal fashion at times, in relation to your use of alcohol. But I want to know more - how did Australya end up like this, Mister Lawson?"

At that moment, a shape loomed outside the window,

emerging momentarily from the clouds north of the house, just above the tops of the trees. It was dark green and yellow, a burgeoning mass, throbbing slowly as it passed.

"A government dirigible," said Bertha.

"Coincidental that it should go over just now," I said. "Perhaps they have noticed that our friend has ceased transmitting."

"Mister Lawson. I have read the terrible history of Europe on my magnetic tapes. I know how humanity came to be what it is. But how did Australya come to be like this? I want to know, and my databases don't tell me. It's all just idle propaganda, lies and half-truths told by party-line historians. Please tell me - you lived through those times - you of all people know how it happened."

A terrible sadness began to come over me, an intense pang of regret, making my stomach sore, and I couldn't bear to tell him that it was all because of my poetry: The Red Revolution's army marching in Faces in the Street, Freedom's on the Wallaby, Past Carin'. I was the one who wrote the soundtrack to Australia's Revolution. My poems inspired the people to rise up and cast off their former masters. The only problem was, the subsequent masters were worse.

I felt a pain in my chest and leaned against the wooden wall of the house rubbing my left breast. I grimaced.

Bertha said, "Are you alright, Harry?"

I said, "I'm fine." My finger brushed at something in my coat - a folded piece of paper. I pulled it out.

It was the pamphlet about Banjo Paterson and Christina, the one that I had looked at the day that this whole story started.

I still had it in my pocket.

I pulled it out and unfolded it and gave it to the Robot.

"This will explain it to you," I said. "This pamphlet tells exactly what it was like."

CHAPTER 11

KONTINUAYSHUN AND REETURN

Well, things went on much the same for about four or five months, with Bertha going to work and me sitting in the house, trying to think up poems, trying not to think of drinking. It was probably the most contented time we ever had.

No, it was definitely the most contented time I had ever had, in my entire life. (What I remembered of my childhood, it wasn't that contented - but they were just memories, anyway. You can't be sure of anything can you? I mean, memories can deceive you - they're not always accurate.) I remember thinking to myself that I had never been so contented.

But like everything good, it eventually came to an end.

It was four-o'clock in the afternoon on a Tuesday, I remember; we had gotten used to the old way of telling the time and date, and the Maori had even found us a twelve hour clock to put on the mantlepiece. Ever since then I have never been able to get to sleep without the sound of a clock ticking somewhere in the house.

I heard a knock at the door, and I remember looking up to see if it was Bertha coming back. That's how I know what time it was.

"Come in," I said.

It was the thin-faced government man, the same one who had brought us here, in his black suit, his gaunt, skeletal hands fiddling restlessly.

Bertha followed him in, saying, "The Maori found him wandering up the track a few miles."

"Got lost, I'm afraid," he said. "The track's gotten a little overgrown this winter." I looked out. The dray horse was tied to a tree, and the cart was looking a little worse for wear, with mud right down one side, all along the wheel and above it. "Almost got the wheel bogged, too. Probably need new tire metal - the strip got twisted when the Maori pulled it out." His face was pinched, lemon-puckered, as though the very effort of existing tasted sour.

Bertha pulled out a chair and said, "Sit down Mister -"

"Mister Adler. Call me Karl."

"I'll get you a cup of tea," I said, and took the kettle off the wood stove. I made a potful, and brought over three cups and a milk jug.

"Aah, thankyou," he said, sipping almost contentedly. "My Marx, you must be glad to see me. First white man you would've seen for a while I would warrant."

Bertha pursed her lips and said, "Mister Adler, we are quite contented here, I can assure you. The Maori have taken to us, and we are regular guests of theirs; indeed, since there is no alcohol here it has been a restful time indeed."

"Yes," said Mister Adler. "The Maori can be terrible when they're drunk."

"Actually, no," said Bertha, "I was thinking of my husband."

Mister Adler fiddled uncomfortably with his collar. "Ahem. In any case, you must be yearning to get back to civilization? Aren't you? Miss the comforts of a proper city? Running water, electricity, people everywhere, places to go, etcetera etcetera?"

Bertha and I looked at each other. What was he getting at?

"We're fine here, Karl," I said. "We both like it."

He stood up and wheeled around on his heels, facing the window that looked out onto the bush. "Nice view," he said. "The thing is, Mister Lawson," he turned around and leaned on the table with the fingers of both hands flatly splayed out, staring rather rudely at me from a higher vantage point, "The thing is, they want you back. Don't know why. Something about difficulties with knowing what you're doing out here - something about the radio reception - I didn't follow all the reasons. But it seems they really want you to be writing... helpful articles... again. And obviously, being so cut off from everything, there is no possible way that you can do that here. As you already know, you need to be in touch with the news to know what to write about. A knowledge of contemporary events is absolutely essential."

"Do we have to go back? What if we refuse?" I asked.

"Refusal may offend, Mister Lawson. Greatly. People whom you do not wish to offend." He spoke in a clipped, left-wing accent, the type that educated Australyuns put on after the ascension of the Marxians.

Bertha started clattering loudly as she cleared away the cups and spoons.

"And don't even think of going behind the lines. Sometime soon we'll be... sending people in to... take care of any reactionaries that might be hiding with the Maori."

I mouthed, "Sutton," and he must have seen the word on my lips, for he said, "Yes, Sutton. Get your things packed. You're going now. And you know, I'm surprised at you, Mister Lawson. I would have expected that you, of all people, might have taken a... politically correct view of things. But even you seem to have been... infected... by the reactionaries. How very strange. I'm sure your superiors will love to know about this."

I stood up and raised myself up so that I towered above him. He was really a rather short man. I looked over my moustaches at him. "I am Henry Lawson, Hero of the Revolushyun; A Trusted Mayt; and one of the Fabyulus Foundas of F.R.E.A.K.IN Australya! Who do you think you are, talking to me this way? You are a nothing - a flea - some lower echelon security lackey, clinging to the coattails of a mid-level nobody like a leech hanging off somebody's bum."

He didn't seem too perturbed, which was a worry. It probably meant he wasn't quite as lower echelon as I thought. "Why, then, Mister Lawson, considering you are such an important person, you would be eager to return to your tasks serving the Revolushyun, writing magazine and newspaper articles praising the Peepl's Power."

Bertha clattered extra loudly and marched out into the

bedroom. "Where's she going?" he snapped.

"To pack I expect," I said, resigned. I sighed. There was nothing we could do.

The Robot just stood there watching. He didn't go in to help Bertha pack, just stood there. I suppose he realised that she needed to do something, or else she might blurt out some politically unacceptable statement.

CHAPTER 12.

THE FIX

The trip back across the Tasman seemed rushed. We were back in our old house in no time and Bertha was becoming very depressed. It seemed as though the entire trip had been cut unnaturally short - we hadn't even had time to say goodbye to our Maori friends - they would surely be wondering what had become of us.

It didn't bode well for the next lot of teachers, actually, I remember thinking.

Bertha spent most of her time staring at the walls. She needed me, and I suppose that's what stopped me drinking for the first month or two. The Robot did the house-work, all of it, and I went to work and came home, and we ate whatever he put on the table in front of us. It was strange how we had come to rely on him. He knew us both, I suppose - he had worked out what we needed. Bertha didn't eat much. She just picked at her food. She was looking pale; her complexion was ghostly and there were rings under her eyes. I don't think she was sleeping much either.

Neither was I.

Then one day at work the Direktor called me in. He was wearing his bullshit face, the one he always wore when he was about to tell someone a bare-faced lie.

He said to me, "Oh, Lawson, the Robot maintenance department going to come around to pick up your Robot. They're going to fix him." The way he said 'fix,' accentuating it unnaturally, made it sound like something more permanent than routine maintenance. "Apparently the... um... automatic diagnosis mechanism is faulty. He needs to be fixed," he accented it again "it's - ah - memory mechanism - something about the Aetheric Pattern or cameratronic something or other. They'll bring back another one if they can't finish the job - so don't worry, you won't be without your Robot for long."

I tried not to rush at the end of the day. I packed everything up slowly and carefully, and dawdled at the entrance talking. I didn't want the Direktor to see how worried I was. But as soon as I got home, I turned the radio on, loud, and gestured to Bertha and the Robot to come into the kitchen.

I wrote on a piece of paper:

Robot - READ THIS! - you are to be taken in for maintenance - government men coming… They are going to wipe out your memory, and put back in the cameratronic mechanism. Make a run for it! Quick! Get away!

For a moment the Robot read it quietly, neither moving nor speaking - I think he had trouble reading my handwriting, actually. But then suddenly and silently I saw the realisation hit him. He turned to me and nodded, collected together a few possessions (several books Bertha and I had given him for his 'birthday', the anniversary of his arrival in the house) and ran quietly out of the front door. I quickly deposited the piece of paper in the oven, went into the other room and turned the radio off, and made a cup of tea for Bertha and I.

The doorbell rang at about Foreteen O-Klok, as dusk was falling (or six o'clock in the old parlance - I got to be quite good at converting) There were four technicians armed with some fairly serious looking utensils, weapons and tools, perhaps for subduing unco-operative Robots.

"May we come in?" they asked. "We are here to collect your Robot."

"I'm sorry, but we can't find our Robot," I said. "I sent it down to the corner store to pick up some groceries about an Our ago. The radio was on rather loudly - I think it misunderstood my instructions. I gave it the list but it should have been back by now, it definitely should. You're welcome to wait until it returns?"

They waited for more than an Our, but of course the Robot

failed to come back. We were most apologetic and they handed me a business card and said, "We hope you get your Robot back soon. If he comes back, call us immediately on this number. He has dangerous, life-threatening faults in his mechanical innards - faults that, if they are not fixed immediately, could endanger your lives. He could blow up at any time, he is a walking time-bomb."

"Oh dear, that's awful," said Bertha and I and accepted the cards.

Bertha took out the dishes and did the washing up rather loudly.

"What's wrong, love?" I said, picking up a teatowel and drying up for her.

"You just got rid of our Robot," she said. "What were you thinking."

I said, "Well, his life was in danger. At least, if not his life, his identity. His mind was about to be wiped."

"Harry, they aren't human. No matter what you think, they're machines. Yes, they might have these 'Aetheric Patterns' Sutton was so keen on - but I don't think in any stretch of the imagination that anyone could honestly say that's the same as a soul. It's a manufactured thing, a machine... You've been telling me things aren't the same at work - now they'll be even more suspicious. And now I'll be saddled with all the housework as well. Remember how horrible that week was without the Robot in Marx Zealand? You're anthropomorphizing a machine. It would have been very easy to get him replaced - now we'll have to save up for another one. And they're suspicious of us now, as well."

My stomach churned as Bertha was saying this - didn't she see the soul staring out of his eyes? Didn't she understand? I thought she understood. After all, she was the one who had drawn it to my attention.

I panicked. I had always thought Bertha was my soul-mate - I realised that for months we had been thinking at cross purposes. We didn't understand each other at all. I thought to myself as I glared at her, she doesn't understand me at all. She was racing around in a manic fit, dusting all the surfaces with a feather duster.

"Damn it, Harry, look at all the housework. The Robot usually does the clothes tonight, and now I'll have to do it. And he sweeps the floor, and look at all the dirt those workmen traipsed in. It's all your fault, Harry. All your fault! It would have been so easy to just leave it - just let them take him - get another one - but oh, no, you couldn't do it." She burst into angry tears.

"I'll help, Bertha. I didn't realise. I thought you understood - I thought you were my soul-mate, Bertha. I thought you saw that the Robot had - human feelings. It was obvious - I thought anyone could see it in his eyes..."

She gave me a look of contempt, or at least, that's what I thought it was at the time. I'm not so sure that it was, now, thinking back on it.

It might have actually been fear of the situation we were in, for I was a marked man now - perhaps she was covering up how afraid she was of the fall in our political standing by talking about housework. She probably wanted me to be strong. To take the initiative. To be a man, and protect us both, get us away. And she had a point. I am sure that, to the Direktor I was persona non grata now, politikally inkorrect.

But at the time I had thought it was a look of contempt and it upset so much that I walked straight out the front door and slammed it behind me.

I found myself down at the Writer's Club. It wasn't what it used to be, but there were one or two writers there still. Mostly it had become the haunt of public servants from the Department of Public Literatur and Re-Edukayshun.

I went in there and sat down at one of the tables. A few of the fellows saw me there, and one of them came and joined me, Frank, Frank Kenna I think was his name. He was a minor writer back in the days of the Bulletin.

"Would you like a drink, Harry? You look as though you might need one."

"Hello Frank. No - look, I've given up drinking. The wife doesn't like it."

"My wife doesn't like me being here much either, Harry. Having problems, are you?"

"You know, Frank, I thought I'd married a soul-mate. But all she cares about is not having to do the chores. She just doesn't understand me, Frank."

He sipped his drink. "I gave up years ago, Harry," he said, and wiped his brow. "We don't talk much. And as far as the marital duties go - well, she don't want to do that either these days - and I don't mean the sweeping. Put it this way - she doesn't want me stoking the fireplace any longer." He sighed and looked me in the eye. "Come on, Harry, just one. One won't hurt. You can stop after that and go home."

I reflected for a moment. He was right - why couldn't I control myself? Just one drink, and then I'd go home.

After that, the night was a blur.

CHAPTER 13.

MORNING AFTER THE NITE BEFOR

I woke up with my head laying in a gutter and levered myself up and caught a taxi home. Didn't have any cash on me, so I gave the taxi driver a poem for the fare. He looked at it and said, "What's this?"

I said, "I'm Henry Lawson. This is a poem."

"Henry Lawson. Who the bloody hell is that? I can't buy diesel with this."

"I'll go in and get some money."

Bertha was sitting on the couch, staring at the door with bloodshot, black-ringed eyes and untidy hair, like a magpie's nest sitting on her head. She looked sick, just the same as she had looked when we had come back from Marx Zealand, only worse. Paler, almost shocked or surprised or something like that, as though she simply couldn't believe what was happening.

I looked at her, but she stared past me, consciously or unconsciously I couldn't say.

I found my wallet in yesterdays trousers and went and paid the taxi driver. Funny thing, I had more money in my wallet now, after being teetotal for more than a year, than I ever had before, when I was a drunk. The thought made me feel miserable and sick. I was a drunkard again, a God-forsaken, dismal, pathetic drunkard.

I went in and sat next to Bertha. She was in a bad state.

"What's happening to us, Harry?" she asked me.

I could only shake my head.

"You have to stop drinking. Don't have another drop."

"I can handle it, Bertha. I just have to make sure I only have one or two. I can do it." I don't even know why I said that.

"You can't handle it, Harry. You never could handle it. Even a drop is too much for you. Can you remember what you did last night, Harry? Don't you remember?"

I couldn't. But a woman was not going to tell ME what to do.

I tramped into the bathroom and had a cold shower, then I dressed in fresh clothes and went out into the kitchen.

Bertha was sitting at the table weeping.

I sat down next to her, put my arm around her shoulders and whispered, "I'm sorry, possum."

"No, Harry. I'm sorry. It was my fault - I drove you to it. I drove you to drink."

She wept disconsolately, then gave several pitiful sobs.

Finally she stopped weeping, exhausted of grief. But then, in such a desolate, empty, dispirited voice that it chilled my soul, she stated, "It's the end of everything, Harry. It's the end of our marriage, it's the end of our lives together. We've tried, we've done our best, we've managed for months, but the demon drink has taken over again."

She began to sob again, but her eyes gave forth no tears, and that was the most tormenting thing to watch. I wanted to promise that I would never drink again, but I felt as though I couldn't make any more promises. Her voice cracked, "There's a grief so great that you have no more tears to cry." Then she wailed, and I gasped at the sound of it. It took her a minute to get control of herself. Nothing I could have said could have helped.

After that sound the noises of traffic and dogs barking outside seemed insufferably quiet.

She finally said in a very small voice, "If you ever drink again, Harry, I'll leave you."

I realised that I didn't want to promise anything, because I knew that once I got drinking, promises meant nothing. Instead I said something I knew patently wasn't true, "Possum, I really can handle one or two drinks. Don't worry."

She rolled her eyes and laughed a bitter, sad laugh.

"What is it, Harry? Why on earth was it the Robot that sparked this binge off? What is it about them that touches something so deep inside of you that it undoes all the hard work we've done to get you off the booze?"

I felt that it was all meaningless - analysing it. I knew that it just was what it was. I am a drunkard, and I can't fix myself. I am what I am. But I said, anyway, as though it might help if we could both fool ourselves into thinking there was an explanation, "I have to know, Bertha. There are mysteries here - where do the Robots get their Aetheric Patterns from? Bertha - you were the first person to mention it - you were the one who noticed it first. And you were right - I know those Robots have souls. I know OUR Robot does. There's a person in there, stuck inside that metal shell. And there's something dark and horrible going on - I don't know what it is - the Maori were right - there's something deep and mysterious and wrong that I don't understand - the Robots are part of a sickness at the heart of our civilisation here in F.R.E.A.K.IN Australya. There is a grub, eating at the fruits of our civilisation, a worm, at the very rotten centre of it, and I want to know what it is and what it means."

Where that speech came from, I didn't even know...that I felt that. That's what the demon drink does to your mind; it changes you so that you don't even know yourself any more, what you're doing or who you are.

Bertha held my hands in her little hands, and it almost made me weep to feel how small they were, around my large hands. "Harry - if that's what you have to do, then that's what you have to do. I don't understand it," she said, looking away. "I don't understand it at all," she repeated. I began weeping pathetically.

"Harry," she said, "You have to do what you have to do. Find out what's going on. For God's sake, Harry, you're a journalist. Remember, you covered the shearing strikes. You found out what was going on then. Find out now. If you think something's going on. Everyone deserves to know - your pamphlets have been telling everybody how free they are - when it's you that needs to know the truth. About this. About a lot of things. But I don't understand why we can't just be happy and forget about all of it. And I don't understand why you can't just stop drinking. Harry, it's all about truth, isn't it?"

And I wept even more.

Truth. Bitterly, I wept. It was the last thing I had cared about. I had already traded in the truth for my own comfort.

"It's not too late for you, Harry," she said, "Perhaps it's too late for us, though. I think it might be."

And she packed her bags and left me.

CHAPTER 14.

INVESTIGAYSHUN AND THE PLANT

After a night of not sleeping, I got up early and went to work.

As soon as I got to work I made an appointment to go to the plant where they make Robots, ostensibly for propaganda purposes. The Boss was pleased, actually, as our Robot technology surpasses the technology of the Reactionary countries by some decades. Well, it does, according to the official point of view. Although I've heard on the grapevine that they're actually doing better than us in Europe, but I would never have dared suggest so in my pamphlets.

I was invited to the Robot Manufacturing Plant the very next day.

Professor Dominica Rossum herself was standing waiting for me at the reception desk; she was the head scientist of the team that designed the Robots and the person who runs the entire project. A tall, severe woman, wearing a grey suit and small, thick spectacles, with long, spindly fingers that spidered out of square, uncompromising knuckles, wearing her hair tightly bound, with pursed lips and pale, sunken, sun-starved cheeks, she was clearly a hard working woman, a product of the Revolushyun and a supporter of the status quo.

She greeted me with a handshake, and said, "Mister Lawson, I know why you're here."

I was surprised by this - how could she know? Could Bertha have informed on me? She was the only one who knew why I was there.

"Yes, Mister Lawson," she continued, "You wish to know about origins. Man today believes he is nothing more than a machine - a biological machine, yes, but a machine. A machine made according to principles of evolution, which is nothing more or less than a blind engineer that shapes each individual for the sole

90

purpose of the survival of the species. Here, we have made more perfect men."

We began our tour - if you could call it that - really, what I saw could be summed up in one word: Mechanical. We followed a large conveyer belt through all the places where the Robots were assembled, where the metal shells received their innards, then to where the legs and arms were attached, then to the part of the factory where the top was bolted on and the head was attached.

I felt strangely sad watching them being made - as if some sacred mystery had been violated. Robot was my friend - he did not seem like a creation of man - at least, not in what he was himself. Yes, his parts all seemed symmetrical and well-ordered, like any engineered thing, but the sum of those parts - what I assumed was the effect of the Aetheric Pattern - his personality - that was another thing. That part of him seemed almost divine - the humanity of the Robot - the soul - and I couldn't seem to come up with any other way of seeing it...

"Professor Rossum," I said, "What about the Aetheric Pattern? What is it that makes them so human in their thought patterns?"

My question clearly caught her off guard; she stammered and stuttered her way through her answer. "Human? They're not hu-hu-human.... Anyway, where on earth did you hear that term, Aetheric Pattern? That doesn't sound like anything I have ever heard of." She looked at me strangely and almost choked out the last phrase. I was sure it was a lie. "Stay here. I must go on ahead and... prepare things for you, Mister Lawson."

"Call me Harry, please," I said, but she simply looked at me uncomprehendingly as she walked away.

Not knowing what to do now I sat down on a nearby diesel supply pipe, that ran beneath a large machine whose purpose I had no clue.

One of the girls working on the assembly line finished her shift and came over and sat near me. I felt a little self-conscious sitting there, actually, because she must have wondered what I was doing, so I simply concentrated on the view of the assembly line that I had.

She ate her lunch quickly and quietly, without saying anything, but after she had finished she turned to me and said quietly, "Excuse me, Mister, but you wouldn't be Henry Lawson would you?"

I admitted that I was. She continued, "My name's Hannah Thornburn, Mister Lawson - I don't usually work on the assembly line but we're short on hands today - I'm a chemical engineer, actually. I've read your work - no, no, not the propaganda - your real work, Mister Lawson - the poems you had published before the Revolushyun. And your journalism..."

Hannah shook my hand firmly - nothing warms my heart more than to meet one of my admirers - and she was certainly an admirer that could warm the heart. She was good looking, with flushed pink cheeks like a girl from Tasmania or the Blue Mountains, delicate, poetic features, bright, lively green eyes and a mouth that almost seemed to pout but didn't. She was slight yet not too skinny, in a prim and trim work dress, but her way of wearing it made it seem as poetic as a princess' wedding dress on any other girl.

She leant close to me, so close that I could feel the warmth of her breath on my cheek. She whispered, "Mister Lawson, there is a coffee shop just across the road from the factory. Meet me there at Thirteen-Seventy O-Klok - that's when my shift ends - and I will tell you... things about the factory that you didn't know." And then, like a frightened possum in the night, surprised by a torch-wielding bushman, she disappeared into the strange, tangled depths of the factory.

Professor Rossum returned presently and I had the distinct impression that the course of our tour had changed direction. The parts of the factory that she showed me were much less interesting even than the places we had already seen. The workers' tea-kitchen, the management meeting room, and the creche where mothers could leave their children during the day, filled with squalling babies crawling over one another. "We are a modern employer, Mister Lawson, and since the One Child Policy began in Australia we have tried to make things easier for working mothers - after all, it might be the only chance they have to have a child, and their children are very precious to them."

The tour ended and I made my way out of the factory. I took a slightly circuitous pathway through the nearby streets until I got back to the coffee shop Hannah had mentioned. It was about Thirteen-Sixty-Three when I got there.

Hannah arrived at Thirteen-Eighty and I bought her a cup of coffee. She put three sugars in, and I said, "But Miss Thornburn, I would have thought you were sweet enough already..."

She said, "Mister Lawson, you are a married man." But she said it with a twinkle in her eye.

"Bertha doesn't understand why I'm here, Hannah. She doesn't really understand why I need to know about the Robots. It's because - "

Hannah nodded, "I understand why you're here. And I know more about the Robots than I can tell you in this public place, Mister Lawson. Do you see that man sitting there? He's what we call a plant - one of the General Sekuriti at the factory - government agents, Mister Lawson, pretending to work in the factory, but their real purpose is to keep an eye on us. I cannot tell you anything in front of him."

"Call me Harry."

Hannah leant close again and whispered, "Mister Lawson, ask me out on a date. I know you're a married man, but perhaps people might be able to understand why a man might want to go out with me, even if he was married. That will give us an excuse to see each other again, and then I will tell you everything that I know."

I cleared my throat. I felt a little awkward and said quietly, "Hannah, would you like to -" but she interrupted, "Mister Lawson, Harry, for goodness' sake I want the security man to hear it. Say it louder."

I said loudly and rather uncomfortably, "Hannah, you're clearly a very... good-looking, appealing girl. Would you like to meet me at a mutual... um restaurant this Fiveday night for dinner?"

She said, "I'd love to, Mister Lawson. Why, thankyou. Might I suggest Evana's, in Swanston Street?"

"Certainly," I said, feeling more confident. "What time would you like me to pick you up?"

CHAPTER 15.

HANNA

I would have never thought I might betray Bertha, not in a million years, but when the opportunity came up I turned out not to be the person I thought I was. Sometimes I think we humans have an infinite capacity for self-deception, and I thought it was just a poetic moment, a moment of love, but the affair with Hannah was a symptom. A small glimpse of the truth about my life. A life in which everything was wrong and I didn't even know it. Every single thing.

I picked Hannah up from her townhouse in a taxi at Sixteen-Ninety O-Klok on Fiveday and the driver reached Evana's in no time. It was a swank silver and napkins place, and I opened the door for her to get out of the car.

We asked the waiter for a secluded corner and he nodded without a smirk. We were tucked away in a corridor, the only table there, but we were still in line of sight of the rest of the restaurant, unfortunately.

Or fortunately, for Hannah said, "Mister Lawson, forgive me, but we need to put on a bit of a show for the other patrons. I believe I recognise one of the security men from the factory is sitting at that table on the left."

"I expect Professor Rossum is having me followed," I said glumly. "I asked some uncomfortable questions at the factory."

I hadn't really clicked on to what she meant by a show.

Hannah leaned forwards and left a lingering, soft kiss on my lips.

I sighed a broken, guilty, hopeful sigh. She moved her chair closer, and kissed me again, more passionately. I felt her whole body responding as I kissed her back. Her left hand was gently resting on my left thigh and my right hand was in the small of her back.

She felt as fragile as a tea-set in my arms, but so soft.

"Ahem." The waiter was standing there.

I came to my senses. The kiss was a betrayal. I couldn't fool myself that I hadn't felt it. I felt shocked by how easy it had been to betray Bertha.

Then I remembered that Bertha had gone. She had left me. But we were still married, weren't we? Were we? I searched my soul, and it seemed to me in that moment that in heart of hearts my marriage felt just as wrong as this did.

But Hannah was so beautiful, she was like a visual poem - as though that justifies anything. Strange how what you see with your eyes can make you blind, blind to the consequences of your actions, blind to your self. Everything in my life was a mess and I just needed... A drink. Hannah was like a drink, for me, a way to forget.

Hannah ordered dinner for both of us. Then she turned to me and said, "If we hadn't done that, Mister Lawson, I have no doubt the security men would have been on our backs all night. Nonetheless, we're not out of the woods yet. We will need to go for a walk after dinner, and put on another... show, I think..."

"Will it be a show?" I asked. Her unfathomable grey eyes were as mysterious as the mists on the Blue Mountains, but she squeezed my hand under the table. I didn't think that gesture was an act for the theatre guests.

I declined to drink that night.

I was drinking Hannah.

Funny, for a relative stranger I could put away the demon drink, but not for my own weary, tired, long-suffering wife, or that's what I thought of Bertha at that guilty moment. Luckily, or unluckily, Hannah didn't have a drink either, or else I might have been inclined to have one myself.

We walked down Swanston street. A block away was Hegel Gardens, a sweeping Victorian era park with elms, poplars, oaks and cedars, surrounding the Worker's Exhibition Hall. (Before the Revolushyun it was called Carlton Gardens and the hall, the Royal Exhibition Hall. No garden quite so poetic has ever been made since.) We wandered into the gardens. A still moon and mists lingering above the waters lent the scene a gentle, soft light.

There were silver swans swimming in the moon-shadow haunted pond. I looked at Hannah - she gazed back at me with a soul as pure as... well, but what we were thinking of doing wasn't pure.

I remember wondering if the worry-lines of my age showed in the moonlight.

"Harry," she said, "You feel it too, don't you?"

She leant her head against my chest. What I could feel was my own heart thumping like a frightened rabbit.

We kissed again, and then she led me to a park bench.

"Hannah," I said, troubled, "You know that I'm a drunkard."

"You're a poet," she said, touching my greying hair so gently. Her voice was rest and relief to my troubles, that night, as it ever was since then too. "You drink because the pain of life is too much. I understand that."

That was the night of our love. She was as beautiful as a moon-shadow flickering in the pond, a white swan.

Then, in each others arms, as I puffed my pipe she said, "Harry, I worked part-time as a secretary at the factory when the Robot manufacturing was started. I know where Professor Rossum's papers are kept. The research papers, from when she was developing the Robots. We can go and find them. We can find out what's really going on. There's something deeply wrong in Australya, Harry. A sickness at the heart. There's something wrong about the way they make the Robots. You know it, you feel it. I know you do. There's a deep, dark secret that they don't want anyone to know about."

We caught a taxi back to her townhouse and I stayed the night there. God knows, sometimes I wish I hadn't done it. Things might still be the same. I might still be living with Bertha, on and off, struggling with my drunken habits, trying to make a life. And Hannah. Hannah would be alright, too. It was that betrayal, my betrayal of Bertha with Hannah, that changed everything, for the worst, for everybody. Especially me.

CHAPTER 16.

THE REESERCH PAPERS

For three weeks our affair continued, sometimes under the watchful gaze of the security men, sometimes away from the world.

I didn't hear from Bertha at all, and assumed she had gone to her mother's place in Marx. She didn't call in at home at all, although I didn't spend a lot of time there, but I dropped in every few days, and there was no sign of her having been there.

Then one night, when Hannah and I were in Hannah's bed, a night when the traffic outside was loud and the radiogram was blaring, Hannah whispered that it was nearly organised. She had found a driver and a car to bring me to the place where the facts would be made clear.

So we arranged to meet the following night, after we had both finished work.

Usually we met at her house. We had decided that Hannah would come to my house for the meeting, though. She knew Bertha had left me, and we both thought it better that we didn't do the same thing as usual, to keep the security men on their toes.

The day at work passed slowly. Every moment of it was longing for Hannah, thinking about Hannah, worrying and obsessing about what I was going to find out.

She arrived early, about Fourteen Sixty O-Klok.

We kissed and I said, "We don't need to do this, Hannah."

She looked upset, pouted and said, "You don't want to kiss me?"

"Of course I do," I laughed. "How could anyone not want to kiss you? You're extremely kissable, love. Eminently kissable. That's not it. We don't need to find about the Robots. We can leave it if you would rather. Perhaps it's better to leave sleeping dogs to lie..."

"Harry," she said forthrightly, "We have to know the truth

- you are the one person who can change things, because of who you are - people respect you, Harry. I know that you're a true poet - you feel these things the same way that I do, deeply, passionately, uncompromisingly. You want to know the truth. I know that you do. And this is your chance to find out the truth about the Robots."

Coming from her, the proposition was completely unanswerable. I would have walked to the moon, if I could have, for her. I would have found a way to do it, even if it was impossible. To risk my life on a Reactionary escapade seemed like a small thing.

"We need to find something to do in the meantime," she said. "I've got a friend with a car - he'll pick us up at Seventy after midnight or thereabouts."

We found something to do...

We were dressed again and ready to go, in dark suits and black hats, when the car's horn sounded.

It was a black, shiny Nyumobile. The driver was a Robot with a scarred, bent faceplate - I had never seen one like him. Usually they are taken back to the factory if they're damaged, and you never see them again. We leapt into the back.

The Robot took us through the backstreets and sidestreets, and past the city lanes and buildings, and then right out of the city into the farmland to the north. There was mist everywhere, and we kept an eye out to make sure we weren't followed.

It began to drizzle.

Soon were travelling along a dark eucalyptus-lined highway, without headlights. I assumed the Robot could see in the dark - some of them have infra-red vision sensors.

After a little while I recognised the road. It was the highway to Echuca, and I was nervous about kangaroos at the speed we were going, but we didn't even see any wildlife, much less hit anything, although the Robot swerved slightly once or twice.

We reached the outskirts of Echuca in less than an Our, by which I calculated that we must have been doing more than a hundred and fifty. The Robot took the side-streets, past the town centre and soon we were weaving our way amongst railway yards, workshops and metalworking places. He took it more slowly through the industrial area, and I noticed at some point that he had put the headlights on.

Then the Robot slowed down.

A dark shape loomed before us in the rain, something like a tall, rounded pyramid, with a truncated top. As we came closer I saw that it was a sawmill. There were neat piles of cut timber around and other piles of sawdust with water rolling down the sides of them in dusty globs and settling in dark, reflective puddles on the mud.

The car bounced across a dirt track that went past the mill, through a small break in the fence at the back, and we found ourselves in a train junkyard, threading our way between piles of railway timbers, old engines, wheels and rusted boiler parts. We seemed to be keeping to the shadows, he was driving very slowly now and the headlamps were off.

"We have to get out here and walk," said Hannah. She had an umbrella and the Robot took it and held it above us; he didn't seem to care if he got wet. I wondered if they get rusty. He walked behind us in the rain and Hannah led the way, between rusting piles of metal parts and giant, dominating, forgotten locomotive engines.

There was a tiny wooden hut at the back of the junkyard, a shed, with a padlock on the door. She had a key and let us in.

It was dry inside. The wooden floor sounded hollow. "It's bigger than it looks. There's a room underneath," she said. "That's where the documents are stored."

She found a trapdoor in the floor, and we clambered down a tiny ladder. It seemed too flimsy for the Robot so he stayed where he was, like a battered sentry, a toy soldier standing on guard.

The air was close and musty in the basement. I had brought a torch with me, and I shone it around. We were in a small dugout room with the roof, the floor of the shed, supported by wooden beams. There were three rows of old, dusty wooden filing cabinets as well as several bookshelves holding documents, books and files. On one side of the room there was a barred window at the top, with darkness outside and rain and mud clattering onto it. The room seemed more solid than the building above, as though it had been built to last.

"They keep the documents here because if there's ever an investigation into the factory they don't want their sins to be exposed," she said. "Of course they're protected by the government at the moment, but these people are paranoid, Harry. And rightly so. It's a scandal - what you're going to read about here - it's a real scandal. Harry, I want you write it up and let everybody know."

Hannah found a switch and an electric lightbulb hanging from the planks of wood above us flickered into life. "I think we're safe with the light on, Harry; it's raining so heavily no one will see it shining from this basement, even if they're looking for it."

A thought suddenly struck me. "Is the Robot -?"

"He has had his cameratronic device and microphone removed - he had an accident once, got run over by a train, that was what caused that derailment a few years back, and the authorities think he was destroyed afterwards. He's safe."

The filing cabinets were locked but Hannah had the key to those as well. "I had these keys copied when I was working here, initially because I thought I might forget to take my keys home one night and get locked out. But I kept them, once I realised what was going on."

She started flicking through files. She gave me one. "This one - it will tell you about the beginning of Dominica's research into Aetheric Patterns. Reading it is pretty hard going, Harry - this was written very early, when the first purges were going on - they hadn't even revised the spelling yet."

"It's alright," I said. "Remember, I grew up with the traditional spelling."

AETHERIC PATTERNS AND RIEMANNIAN GEOMETRY
DR. Dominica ROSSUM

Presented at the Particle Physics and Brain Institut conference, Sydney.

In this research paper I intend to outline the experimental outcomes of our enquiry into Aetheric Patterns and their possible relationship with the known geometric structure of Space-Time. Following on from Einstein's theory of relativity, we have formed a theory that the structure of space-time requires additional dimensions, for the square of distance equation that represents clearly two neighbouring points $ds^2 = dx_1^2 + dx_2^2 + dx_3^2 - dx_4^2$ according to Riemann's description of n-dimensional metrical space and Einstein's theory, contains no reference point.

Based on our prior research into the function of the brain we have formed a hypothesis that the brain is not complete in itself but is actually a transmission device that may be compared to a radiogram, forming a connection between what may be called the 'mind', a pattern of energy in the fourth and fifth physical dimensions, and the world of the four dimensions of space and time that we inhabit.

Our experiments were conducted upon social undesirables whose life functions had been interrupted either by an electric shock to the cardiac system or a denial of oxygen. We measured the sum total of electrical brain activity in frequency and voltage and were able to relate this structure to the lingering Aetheric Pattern in the other dimensions after the demise of the patient, using an artificial transmission device, an artificial brain, if you will. The conclusion was that the Aetheric Pattern is real and measurable, and that artificial transmission devices can be created to access the Aetheric

Pattern of an individual after they have died,
in essence, capturing the unique pattern of
energy and frequency and enabling the mind of
the individual to continue relating to four-
dimensional space-time even though their body has
ceased functioning.

Interestingly, not every subject seemed to be
amenable to our research, and we found not a few
whose vital essence could not be captured - we
could not understand why - their Aetheric Patterns
had either disappeared or they had some method
of resistance or protection from the process. At
least 30% were pliant, and that was enough to come
to statistically significant conclusions.

Detailed data and statistics follow.

After this there were pages and pages of equations, numbers,
statistics and charts. But the introduction told me everything I
needed to know.

"It's couched in academic language," I said to Hannah, "But
I see what they were doing. They were killing people and then
capturing their ghosts in some God-damned artificial brain."

"Indeed," said Hannah. "Here, read this." She pulled out a pile
of documents from another cabinet and handed me several pages
stapled together. "It's a letter from Dominica to the Supreme
Marxist Council. In it she's outlining their plans."

Dr. Dominica Rossum
To the Supreme Marxist Council
REGARDING THE PROJECTED POPULATION INCREASE AND A
SUGGESTED SOLUTION

In future years it is projekted that Australya's
population will increase exponentially, partly
due to the inability of peeple to plan for their
retirement when they are unable to earn more than a
set amount of income under Marxist policies. It has
been observed by Hinchley (footnote 2) that they
are already having many more children than before
the Revolution. The suggested enforcement of a One-
Child policy is an integral part of the solution.

However, this will cause another problem. People in their old age will become a burden on the coffers of the state.

Our researches are suggesting a possible solution.

Robots can be constructed using Aetheric Patterns, that are able to understand human instructions and follow them. These can be provided for a reasonable cost to households, and can aid people in their housework and general tasks, as well as providing a rudimentary level of company for the lonely in their old age.

The Aetheric Pattern technology, which we have outlined earlier, requires the termination of other living subjects in order to be properly realised. What we propose is that social undesirables, individuals of Reactionary Tendencies or Bourgeois Mindset, and even those unwanted children, born or yet to be born, that exist contrary to the One-Child policy, be supplied to a euphemistically named 'hospital' where their Aetheric Patterns would be appropriated for the Robots. These Robots would then be provided to the public as a boon, a necessity, to do the work that women would otherwise be forced to do in the home.

This will have the added benefit of supporting our policy of making women independent from male domination.

Hannah was reading it over my shoulder. "So you see, they were already planning to kill prisoners, 'social undesirables,' Reactionaries, and perhaps even children and babies, in order to steal and imprison their souls, essentially, Harry, inside a metal shell. And that's what they did, Harry. The proof is all in here, in these filing cabinets. The Robots are human inside."

"I knew they were human," I said. "I knew it."

Suddenly the sound of dogs barking viciously somewhere

above us filtered through the din of the tapping rain on the windowpanes. The trapdoor in the ceiling opened and the Robot stretched his battered head through the opening and said, "There are people in the junkyard, with dogs, I think they might be government agents. We might need to get out of here quickly."

Hannah grabbed another document and handed it to me. "Put this one in your jacket pocket, Harry - it's important. Read it later - just don't let them catch you with it, that's all."

She switched off the light and we climbed up the ladder.

CHAPTER 17.

ESKAPE

The Robot went to the door and looked out. "It's safe for the moment," he said, and we followed him out.

We could see torchlights in the dark, flicking to and fro, at the far side of the junkyard and the sound of the dogs barking was getting closer. As she replaced the padlock on the door Hannah whispered, "They'll be here soon. Come this way. There's a way out through the back fence."

We had forgotten the umbrella - it was still sitting somewhere in the basement. We were already drenched by the time we had made our way behind the building. We ran through wet, high grass, past a weeping willow, to an old, rotting, dog-legged wooden fence. Hannah continued along until we got to a place where one of the slats was broken. She lifted another plank and it made a space big enough for both of us to get through.

The Robot said, "I will wait here. I'll hold them up. Miss Thornburn - thankyou for what you are doing for us."

"Come with us," said Hannah, beckoning to him.

The dogs barking were getting closer.

"No," he said firmly. "I want the truth to come to light. I want the suffering of Robots exposed. I am prepared to die to fulfil that purpose - I believe that my Aetheric Pattern will find its place in another dimension, Miss Thornburn. This life is not the end for me. I am ready to be a martyr!"

The torchlights were already flickering at the edge of the shed.

"Hurry!" said the Robot, closing the fence slat behind us. I saw him run past, and heard the shouts of the security men chasing him. "Stop! Stop there!"

Hannah grabbed my hand and we slid down an embankment, onto a patch of grass. Further down there was a small jetty with a boat tied up to one of the posts, and Hannah leapt over and untied the rope. She cried, "Quick, get in, Harry!"

I jumped in and helped her to steady herself as she stepped in, then grabbed the oars and pushed us away from the jetty. I rowed for my life, and the jetty gradually moved away.

A large German shepherd came sliding down the embankment, followed by another, then three men jogged down with the light from their torches twitching and jerking along the ground in front of them. One of the dogs leaped into the water and began swimming after us. I rowed as hard as I could to get away, but he was catching up with us.

He reached the boat fairly easily it would seem and snapped at the oar, growling and snarling ferociously. I turned the oar round in my hands and hit at him savagely with the blunt end. The dog panicked, splashing and wetting us with river water. I hit him again and he gave a high whimper and turned around and swam back quickly to the jetty. Suddenly I had to shield my eyes - a bright light was shining on my face. One of the torches on the shore had found me.

"I know who that is!" shouted a voice from the Jetty. "A famous writer - works for Re-edukayshun in Melbourne doesn't he?"

"Are you sure?" said another voice.

"Gut them. It doesn't matter," said a lower, older voice. "That archive is a prohibited space. They're criminals. They wouldn't be running away if they weren't guilty."

Gunshots sounded across the watery expanse, splashing uncomfortably close.

I suddenly found renewed strength for my efforts at pulling the oars and we shot along for a moment, like a steamboat coughing its engine into life. I put every ounce of effort into yanking the oars to and fro, and my arms were aching. The gunshots continued, but they were becoming less accurate as we got further away.

In about half a Minit we rounded a bend in the wide, lazy river, and soon the gunshots stopped and we had lost sight of them entirely. Hannah breathed an audible moan, "Thank God. I thought that was it, Harry."

The rain had stopped and the night was cool and clear. The clouds were somewhere else now, and we drifted along underneath a watchful multitude - the stars - looking down mercifully on our poor, forgotten, forsaken lives.

We removed our wet, soaking clothes and arranged them to dry around the boat.

We both knew, somehow, that this was the end.

Once we got back to Melbourne I could not endanger her by continuing to see her - they knew who I was now. They knew it was me. The pang we felt, of imminent parting, gave our love a sweetness and gentleness that night that it had not known before - we abandoned ourselves to it, without any thought for any consequences. It was too late for that now.

The night seemed to go on and on. But still, it was over too soon.

CHAPTER 18.

BUSH JURNEY

We woke up in the mid-morning, drifting lazily along beneath some old, spindly, splendidly gnarled Mallee trees, with their green tufts shaking gently above us in the breeze.

"Somewhere south of Swan Hill, I would say," said Hannah, rocking the boat as she pulled her dress on rather clumsily. Then she gave a little cough. "I seem to have caught something of a chill, Harry, last night. It will go away soon I'm sure."

"That's no good, Hannah. Take my jacket if you like - try to keep warm."

My clothes were dry, if a little stiff. I put my shirt and trousers back on.

"We probably need to find a place to go ashore," I said.

I rowed the boat ashore and we came to ground on a small, sandy beach, beneath the rotten, pale branches of a sprawling river redgum. The Murray continued flowing past us as I jumped out and pulled the boat further in, jamming it onto the rivergrass. Hannah got out too, pulled her handbag out of where she had stowed it in the prow, then pushed the boat back in to the water. It floated away in lazy circles.

I said, "What did you do that for?"

"If they don't know where we stopped it might be better for us," she said. I watched the boat rotating slowly and freely in the water as it disappeared from view. It made me think of our love, somehow, and I felt sad.

We held hands. "What are we going to do for food?" I asked her.

"Don't worry. I've got this."

She pulled a '38 revolver out of her handbag. "I have twelve bullets."

"And there I was thinking you were such a sensitive, poetic girl," I said.

She coughed again. "That damned cough."

I said, "Why did you bring the gun in the first place?"

"Oh, I thought we might need it. You know, if they captured us." I thought she was joking for a moment, but I don't think she was. She looked very serious, I decided.

Yes, that is poetic, I thought to myself. And a little bit frightening.

She turned out to be a good shot, though, and we had breakfast cooking over a fire in no time, an unfortunate rabbit that had made the mistake of showing its furry face over a log. We buried the rabbit-skin. "Makes it harder for the trackers to find," she said. "They might have trackers on our tail, Harry. Though I think we're safe for a while."

I said, "We'll be harder to find than a needle in a haystack out here. You're a competent young lady, aren't you?"

"Dad wanted to make sure I could take care of myself after the Revolution happened, Harry. Come on, I brought a map and a compass, too. I didn't think anyone would catch us there, but I planned for our escape through the bush just in case. Lucky that I did."

It took us two days to get to the nearest station, but we got there fine. It didn't rain much more, and Hannah's cold seemed to improve a little. We told the station owners we were a married couple who worked painting fences (I had done plenty of that in the past), and we spent a couple of days staying in a shearer's hut there. We knew we had to move on when the station manager received a telegraph about two fugitives, but he was good about it. Country people don't tend to be very fervent about Marxian ideology, actually - he told us they were looking for us and asked us where we wanted to go.

So that was how Hannah and I realised the time had come to part ways.

It turned out to be the last time I ever saw her.

She tried not to weep as we said our goodbyes - she said she didn't want me to remember her with a tear-stained face, but she wept anyway, and so did I, a little, and she coughed as well, for the cold she had developed hadn't gone away. That little cough just went to my heart, and I said, "How can I let you go, Hannah?" We held onto each other for a long, long time.

Finally she left.

Hannah made her way to Adelaide by steamboat where she had some relatives she could stay with for a while, and I accepted a lift back to Melbourne from the station owner, who was taking some stock in to market. I told him I had to work, and that Hannah was going to a little holding we'd purchased in South Australia. I'm pretty sure he didn't believe anything I told him, but it didn't seem to matter.

As we rattled along the country roads my chest was aching terribly, I was almost gasping for breath from the pain of the loss. The farmer drove slower, thinking it was the jolts and bumps of the ride, which it was, in a way, if you see the road as life.

I had only known her for a month. Yet it felt as though my heart had been ripped out of my chest. There was a gaping hole where Hannah had been, a terrible emptiness that promised to last for years and years.

And I knew that as soon as the opportunity might arise to fill up the emptiness with a beer or two I would probably take it.

CHAPTER 19.

TO MARX AND BAK AGAIN

I arrived home to find a telegram from Bertha in the letterbox.

HARRY STOP I HAVE THOUGHT THINGS THROUGH AT MY MOTHERS PLACE AND I REALISED THAT WE CAN STILL MAKE A GO OF OUR MARRIAGE STOP I KNOW HOW HARD YOU HAVE TRIED STOP I AM WILLING TO GIVE YOU ONE MORE CHANCE STOP I WILL BE BACK IN MELBOURNE ON THE THIRTIETH STOP I SINCERELY HOPE YOU WILL ACCEPT ME BACK STOP YOUR POSSUM BERTHA

I felt so many mixed feelings - but mostly guilt and self loathing - as I read the telegram. It was the 20th. She was due back in a Tenday's time.

I went in to work the following day and apologised for being absent. I told the Direktor that I had followed my wife up to Marx because she had left me, and he appeared to accept that. "You ought to give up drinking, Harry," was all he said, and I could only agree with him. I told him I thought she might come back if I went up there again. He agreed, and I went straight to the telegraph office and sent Bertha a telegram telling her to stay in Marx, that I would come up to her. And I ended it with, "Sorry about the tenth. I'll make it up to you."

I caught the train, and was in Marx half a day later.

Bertha met me at the station and said, "What did you mean by, 'Sorry about the tenth?' You weren't even here on the tenth."

"Yes I was, if anyone asks, Bertha, please." I probably should have told her the whole story there and then; who knows, in the end it might have made all the difference? But, sorry to say, I just said, "Possum, I can't tell you the whole story - it would endanger you even to know what's been going on - it's about the Robots but I can't say more than that." I felt like a rotten husband and a cowardly bastard, all rolled into one.

112

She accepted it, though; it reflected much credit on her. She was always a much better wife than I was a husband. Staying in Marx with her mother was something of a strain, though. Her mother mostly refused to speak to me except for necessities, like, "Harry, take out the rubbish," "Harry, you didn't close the dunny door, the redbacks'll get in," or, "Go and get Bertha for dinner, Harry," and whenever I was in the room she seemed to wear a permanent scowl directed at me. And Bertha herself seemed overly happy, in a fey, unnatural way - as though her cheerfulness was a lie - like a light-coloured coat she was putting on to cover the black blouse of despair and grief that she really wore beneath it.

The smile she habitually wore seemed so fragile I thought she might break if somebody merely looked at her the wrong way.

It was a relief when we headed back to Melbourne about a month later. I don't think that month at her mother's did her any good at all, in fact, I think the strain of it caused most of her problems after that.

I went straight in to work and saw the Direktor when we arrived, but Bertha went home. The Direktor said to me after I came in, "Funny thing, Lawson - Sekuriti has been looking for a man who matches your description in the country around Echuca. Broke into an archive or something - they picked up a few swagmen and itinerants but none of the fingerprints matched. If you hadn't been in Marx with your wife, we might have suspected you, you know, because they specifically described him as looking like you. But there you are - thank Marx you have an alibi. Literally."

I took that as a subtle warning, though it may not have been intended as such - in fact, it might even have been his idea of a joke. But I did my day's work and also handed in the report on the Robot factory, which I had honed to the point of political insignificance while I was in Marx, and then I caught the bus home.

When I came through the door Bertha was sitting on the

floor with dishevilled hair and clothes and tear-marks down her face, weeping and howling and staring at me with wild, crazy, hate-filled eyes. On the floor around her were envelopes, torn open, and a bunch of letters in Hannah's handwriting. They must have arrived while we were in Marx.

I helped her up, clumsily helped her over to the lounge chair, onto which she collapsed, howling and speaking gibberish like an insane person. I tried to comfort her for a moment but she actually tried to bite me.

I gathered up the envelopes, which Bertha had neatly arranged on the floor together with their postmarks, and the letters, which were in a mess, and went into the kitchen and started sorting through them and reading them, beginning with the earliest.

I couldn't think of what else to do. I couldn't think of how to comfort Bertha. I wish I had been able to, but I just didn't know what to say or do. It was completely useless.

These were the letters:

Dear Harry

Please remember to read the other documents. I think they might have a bearing on where all this is headed.

You know everything else that I cannot say in this letter, about us. That I wish things were different.

Please remember me.

Don't forget to read the other documents.

Hannah.

114

BY ROBERT DENETHON

Dear Harry

I reached the homestead but my relatives seem to have moved. Health not good - the cough I developed that night on the - ahem - river cruise still has not gone away. Be that as it may, I thank you for the excellent memories. The night at the park, our first night together, was so poetic, beautiful, moonlight, swans, everything was wonderful. I will never forget it. I will never forget you, Harry.

Your love forever and ever, Hannah.

Dear Harry,

Still looking for a place to stay. I managed to find shelter in a Catholic Church last night (Imagine that! Me! Brought up as a Presbyterian) But the priest found me there this morning and sent me packing - I think he thought I was an immoral girl, if you know what I mean.

Which I suppose I am, when I think of what we got up to together.

Your passion, forever, Hannah.

P.S. that cough is still there but I think it might be getting better.

Dear Harry,

Found a place to stay, working as a seamstress. A little draughty, though, and it is not very warm at night. Wish you were here. I will always remember the rapport we found in each other - you are my soul-mate, Harry, my soul, the partner of my spirit. I am your Spirit Girl, Harry. I will guide you. I want to guide you, to help you, to make you stronger. Harry, I beg you, do not turn to drink - remember everything I told you. Hold on to our love.

I truly wish that you were here.

Cough seems a little worse, actually. I am saving up to go to the doctor.

Your eternal lover, your own moon-shadow, reflection of Venus rising in the still waters, Hannah.

Dear Harry

Finally ...!

Saw the Doctor today - it took all the money I might have used for food this week. Never mind - I will be fine I am sure. I am used to not eating much The Doctor told me to go to the hospital immediately, but I will leave it for a few days because I cannot afford the tram fare just yet. Please do not worry about me.

But if you feel inclined you might write to me.

I would love to hear from you, my love. Your voice, your poetry, your laugh. The touch of your hands, your tender touch. I miss everything about you so much. How you worshipped me, my love, with your body.

I know it is just words, on a page, but I would love to have something - some token of your love - that I could hold and treasure and pore over.

Please write to me, Harry, or telegraph me. I am staying at the YWCA hall in Adelaide. It is a bit dingy but its fine - if you simply send the telegram Care Of the Young Womens Christian Association in Adelaide it ought to reach me.

Always Yours,
Hannah.

Dear Harry

I am in Hospital.

The nurse tells me that I have Tuberculosis - I simply cannot believe it as I do not feel ill enough to be that sick. She told me to make my will as well, something that is rather disconcerting as you *can imagine, but I expect they tell that to all the patients.*

Nonetheless, my cough has worsened somewhat - in fact, it is a rather hacking cough now. On the one hand I would not want you to see me when I am in the midst of the coughing spasms but I do so wish to see you. I must rest now. Please remember

I love you.

Hannah.

The last letter was speckled with blood.

Dear Harry,

Not feeling so well often in pain.

I love you. Still waiting to hear from you tho

I do not know why you have not even sent a telegram. Perhaps back with your wife? Waiting

You could still send me a telegram.

Love always. Forever.

Your only love, forever.

Hannah XO

Bertha was still wailing in the room next door. It was making my head ache.

I should have done something about Bertha, but I didn't. Instead I ran out the laundry door and sprinted up the street to the local Post Office, which was already closed, but I bashed my fist on the door knocker until somebody opened it.

I shouted, "I must send an urgent telegram!" The postman was going to send me off with a choice word or two, I'm sure, but I think he recognised me and thought better of sending a 'Hero of the Revolushyun' packing. Instead he let me in saying, "Make it quick. It's past closing time and I'm late for dinner. My wife's going to kill me." I laughed a bitter laugh at that.

I told him to send the following telegram to the hospital.

HANNAH THORNBURN STILL LOVE YOU COMING AS SOON AS I CAN GET A DIRIGIBLE TICKET LOVE HARRY LAWSON STOP

The man sent it and said, "Yes, Mister Lawson, that has been sent. That is thirty shillings. Alright, if that is all, then..." But the machine in front of him beeped and ticked, and he inked his pen and said, "Wait... there's a reply coming in already. That's unusual, from Adelaide..."

He noted it down and then handed it to me.

"I'm sorry, Mister Lawson," he said, "I really am."

It said:

HANNAH THORNBURN DECEASED TWO DAYS AGO STOP

CHAPTER 20.

CLIF EDJ

I went straight to the Writer's Club and took out Twenty Pounds from my wallet, which really was a large amount in those days, gave it to the bartender and said, "Don't stop serving me until I fall over."

He nodded slightly doubtfully and accepted the money gladly.

I can't remember much in the tavern, except that I was weeping at some point, with my head in my hands, and at another point someone was shouting at me to get out or go away or something.

I remember stumbling drunkenly over the sandhills, past the boulders and the beaches, gazing at the moon reflected in the still, clear ocean as I wandered up along the cliffs. I remember asking God, "Why?" and thinking that if there was a God, such a thing could not have happened. I even remember God answering me in my thoughts, although that was probably just the booze talking, as it does in the worst moments of drunkenness. And Hannah's voice was saying, "I'll be your Spirit Girl, Harry. I'll be your strength."

I remember thinking about suicide. There was a dreadful, dark, hollow feeling in the pit of my stomach, but whether I really intended to do it I can't remember. I just wanted to be with Hannah.

Did I jump, or merely stumble? I don't know. There was a moment of darkness, that's all.

I woke up in the hospital bed. The nurse said, "He's awake already."

The Doctor came in and said, "Your wife was here today, Mister Lawson, but she has gone home again. You're lucky to have survived. You fell at least twenty feet, and we thought you were going to be unconscious for many more days than that. You've been out for three days already, as a matter of fact. And

120

it is quite remarkable, not only that you survived the fall, but that you didn't break your back or your neck. If I was a religious man - as I used to be in the old days - I would say that it was a miracle. You are a very lucky man indeed, Mister Lawson, very lucky indeed..."

I said, "Will you send me home, now, Doctor?"

He said, "No. We'll be keeping you in here in order to observe you for signs of melancholy or depressed spirits for the next week or two at least. Your wife told me what happened, you see. It is a rather terrible thing when a close friend dies, especially when she was like a sister to your wife. That you weren't able to be there to help her and missed the letters she sent you, through no fault of your own, has undoubtedly unhinged your mind, Mister Lawson. But I want you to reassure yourself that time heals all wounds."

Bertha arrived later in the day. She was going to tell me about the fairytale she had told the doctor, but I told her I already knew.

Her mood was unreadable, inscrutable. I felt that if anyone was unhinged, it was Bertha, but I could not do anything about it.

The doctor let me out a week later and I went home.

When I went into the house it was a mess. My books and papers were strewn everywhere, and there was rotting food on the floor and even on the walls, as though it had been tossed there, and Bertha herself was sitting in the middle of the lounge room, babbling to herself in incoherent ramblings, not in any language I had ever heard. She had completely lost herself.

I tried to help her onto the chair, to comfort her, but she merely hit out at me. The room stank of urine.

I picked up the telephone and immediately rang through to the local sanatorium.

They arrived in Ten Minits. Three men wearing white uniforms rushed into the house and dragged Bertha, raving hysterically and clawing at them like a caterwauling cat, out through the door and into the back of a large white van.

Once the van had receded I began to clean up the house.

That afternoon I started off to go to the Writer's Club, but as I set off I thought to myself, what would Hannah think of this? I seemed to hear her say, "Turn around, Harry. Don't go. Stay at home."

I turned myself around and walked back home - and I think it was one of the most difficult things I have ever done. You cannot imagine the effort it cost me.

Instead of drinking that night I wrote a poem.

To Hannah

Spirit girl to whom 'twas given
To revisit scenes of pain,
From the hell I thought was Heaven
You have lifted me again;
Through the world that I inherit,
Where I loved her ere she died,
I am walking with the spirit
Of a dead girl by my side.

Through my old possessions only
For a very little while,
And they say that I am lonely,
And they pity, but I smile:
For the brighter side has won me

By the calmness that it brings,
And the peace that is upon me
Does not come of earthly things.

Spirit girl, the good is in me,
But the flesh you know is weak,
And with no pure soul to win me
I might miss the path I seek;
Lead me by the love you bore me
When you trod the earth with me,
Till the light is clear before me
And my spirit too is free.

Then I sat on the porch and looked at the sunset as it lit the sky a brilliant red. It was a moment of peace and stillness, and somehow it reminded me of Hannah. But it also reminded me of how alone, solitary, lost I was now.

I thought to myself, I have nothing to remind me of her. She is the love of my life, and I have nothing.

Nothing except the letters.

I began reading the letters again. The first one - about the documents - reminded me that the three documents were still in my coat-pocket, and I had not yet read the last document that she gave me.

I found my coat, took the document out and opened it up.

It was shorter than the others, in the modern speling, which was a relief:

```
MEMO TO HEAD OF SIENTIFIK DEVELOPMENT
   Progres report: All experiments going well.
We are just days away from acheeving the goal.
The latest simulaykra actually beleeved he was
human. For a short while he even fooled the doktor
that examined him - the realistik heartbeat was
an ekselent idea - when the doktor inspekted the
eer and mouth and genitals he reelized it was
a simulaykra and not a human being. An amazing
result. The copied Eetheric Patten seems to
adequitly displays the previus Eetheric Pattens.
```

That was all that it said.

If I understood it correctly, it meant that the scientists were not only making Robots - they were also attempting to make human simulacra - things that looked like humans but that weren't - Robots that looked like humans. For a dreadful moment I thought Hannah might be a Robot - but then I remembered that her mouth, her ears and everything else were normal. And Hannah had gotten sick. A Robot wouldn't have imperfections - would they? They never do. They never get sick, they can't get drunk, or fall in love, they never make mistakes, except the kind of mistakes that come from being a machine and not fully human. I wondered why Hannah had insisted that I read the document. What was the terrible conspiracy?

I didn't really get any closer to finding out the answer for several months, during which Bertha recovered enough to come home. She was a broken person now, though, and often seemed listless and uninvolved. Any romance between us seemed impossible; our marriage had died, and I was the one who had killed it.

We were eating dinner one night when Robot returned.

CHAPTER 21.

ROBOT

He came to the laundry door and knocked. Bertha thought it was an itinerant swagman looking for work or some dinner, but he said, "No, it's me."

I recognised the Robot's voice and we welcomed him in. Bertha made him a cup of tea and he sat down and spoke to us.

"Mister Lawson, I know an awful lot about the journey you have been on. A friend of mine was a Robot nurse at the hospital in Adelaide, you see, and she contacted me recently on the underground network. I believe a friend of yours... died in the hospital. She talked to my friend, before she died, and told her the whole story.

"But there is still a piece of the puzzle that you haven't got, a clue that has evaded you. That is why I have come here to see you. We haven't got much time. I want you to come with me - there is something you need to see. The final piece of the puzzle, Mister Lawson, Missus Lawson. The final clue."

Bertha was upset - I am sure she knew that the Robot had been talking about Hannah when he mentioned a friend of mine in Adelaide, so she scowled and said, "You go, Harry. Whatever business this is, I want no part of it. I've had enough troubles in my life lately, Robot. What do I need more troubles for?"

The Robot said, "No, Missus Lawson. It is absolutely essential that you come with us too. And when I say we don't have much time, I really mean it, Missus Lawson. The window of opportunity that I am talking about will close very soon, and then, everything will be lost for your husband. Everything will be lost. You must understand, you have to come as well, Missus Lawson."

Bertha looked at me, as if she was weighing up her alternatives. I felt for a moment as though she was still going to refuse to come, and my heart sagged. But, reluctantly, in a state of subdued melancholy, she went and got her coat and came with us. "I suppose Harry's worth it," she said. "I suppose he is," but she didn't sound as though she really believed it.

The Robot had a car at the back, a black Nyumobile such as the Government often uses, like the one that had taken Hannah and I to Echuca that night. Then I saw that the driver was the very same Robot, the one with the scarred, battered faceplate, the one who had derailed a train.

I greeted him as though he was a long-lost friend. After all, he was the only person I still knew who had also known Hannah. If he was a person - I still wasn't sure if Robots were people then, although I was fairly certain that they were.

Bertha and I got into the back, and our own Robot sat in the front passenger seat.

As we drove our Robot turned his head around and talked. For some reason he was addressing Bertha now, and not me, and it perturbed me not a little. He said, "I am part of the underground, now, Missus Lawson. They have found a way to disable the cameratronic devices and the microphones in Robots. I don't know if... Harry... told you the whole conspiracy." Bertha shook her head. "The government scientists have been putting the souls of condemned political reactionaries, rebel intellectuals, even unwanted children, perhaps even babies, into the Robots. We Robots, Missus Lawson, are the product of the inhuman policies of this government. Just as the Maori said, we bear the souls of deceased persons - that is, the Aetheric Pattern that was appropriated from a dead person - that Pattern which our mechanical minds are made to communicate with. But there are even worse things that they are trying to do. Missus Lawson..." His faceplate took on a conspiratorial aspect, and he whispered, "Missus Lawson... There are people who have disappeared who have been replaced by Robots that look completely human. This is real, it is happening, and it is a conspiracy. These Robots do not even know that they are not human. Yet even so, they are human, for their souls are human." Then he turned to me and said, "I know that you already know all of this... um, Mister Lawson. I just really want to say one thing to you. I am everlastingly grateful to you, Harry, for seeing that I am... human, really... at heart... and for giving me my freedom. For not letting them take away my identity. And... let me say as well... I'm sorry..."

He stopped there, in mid-sentence, and I had no idea what he was trying to say. But we had been driving along Russell street and had passed the Police building and Courthouse, and had come to the Old Melbourne gaol, where the car stopped.

I was about to open the car door and run away, but the Robot put his hand on mine and said, "No, um... Mister Lawson... Please believe me when I tell you that I am not betraying you to the authorities - please believe me. What happens next is completely up to you, Mister Lawson - the future is in your hands, if it is in anyone's. But you must come with me. There is something you need to know, that you must know. And I cannot tell you about it - you have to see it for yourself."

"Why?" I asked.

"Because if you don't see it for yourself you simply won't believe me."

He got out and opened the door for us, then went to the gate. The gate was a Robot, and our Robot talked to it. It let us in, and a Robot guard in the uniform of a prison officer came to escort us through the courtyard. Two heavy iron doors opened and we went in.

There was a policeman sitting at a desk, but the Robot guard said something to him and he waved us through. Our Robot talked to the next gate, heavy with iron bars, another Robot in the form of a gate, and it swung open to let us through.

We walked down a set of stone stairs into a corridor dimly lit by a single flickering lightglobe, flanked on both sides by about twenty heavy iron doors. Each of the doors had a tiny, square barred window half-way up, through which grimy faces could be seen peering out, to see who was disturbing their gloom. And there were small, locked portals near the bottom of the doors, through which I presume food was passed. At the end of the corridor was a door much smaller than the others.

We walked all the way down the corridor to that tiny door. The Robot guard had a set of keys on his belt. He unlocked it and we went through. There was a set of stone steps leading downward into absolute darkness.

The Robot guard's faceplate lifted and a torch shone out from his brow. It hardly seemed to make an impression on the deep darkness of that place, indeed, it was swallowed up in the gloom, but we could see enough of the steps to make our way down to the bottom.

At the bottom was another iron door, without a window in it or a grate or any portal. The Robot guard unlocked it and we followed him in. The ceiling was so low in there that we all had to bend. Even Bertha couldn't stand up straight.

The Robot shone his torchlight towards the far corner of the tiny cell. A man lay there on the rocks, cowering in the darkness, hiding his face from the light.

He removed his hand from his face.

It was me.

CHAPTER 22.

EXCHANJ

Bertha began to stumble around, holding her head with both hands as though her brains were about to explode, and her body was being tossed to and fro by the distress that had taken hold of her. In that tiny cell I feared that she was going to thrash herself against the wall or smash her head on the roof.

She cried out insanely, "But... if you're Harry who have I been living with?"

I was uncomprehending. My mind was reeling. I suddenly realised what she was saying.

She was looking at me as though I was a complete stranger.

She wailed, "Harry... Harry... A double... I'm so sorry Harry. A doppelganger... A monster! I've been living with a monster! Oh God! I had sexual relations with a monster! A blasted Robot! A machine! A lie! Everything's been a lie!" She was shaking pitifully now and pointing at me, her mouth sagging open like that Goya painting. "You... monster! You're a monster! An imitation!"

She ran over to the Henry Lawson chained to the floor. His hollow, sunken, dark-rimmed eyes looked out at her disbelievingly, like an owl staring out of a shadowy hollow in an ironbark tree. Bertha was weeping with rage and stamping her feet and she cried out, "Oh, God, Harry, look at you! I knew that thing wasn't you. You would've given up the drink for me, Harry, I know you would've. You would never have taken up with that witch Hannah like he did... You would have never betrayed me. I know you wouldn't have." Then she glanced back at me with a face so desperately hostile with disappointment that I couldn't believe how much she hated me.

I collapsed onto the ground, holding my own head in my hands, and just lay there, paralysed by the situation. I couldn't think, I didn't know what to think, I didn't know how to cope with it.

A great smile split the real Lawson's face, cracking it open like parched earth in a drought, and he said, "Bertha! I knew you'd realise. I knew you'd come and get me."

I saw the look of consternation pass over Bertha's face in that moment. She hadn't realised, and she knew it very well. But she embraced the real Lawson tenderly, and he kissed her again and again and again. He kissed my wife's eyes - my wife - his wife - again and again.

My head was spinning, I was falling into deep, deep darkness, and the dungeon seemed to be swallowing me alive. I felt as though I was plummeting the wrong way, up into a dark, deep night sky, with no stars, no moon, no light, only it was downwards. I was falling.

She ordered the Robot guard, "Open his chains."

Our Robot spoke up. "Alright. But we can't take both of them with us," he warned. He looked at me.

Bertha said, "We're not."

I wondered what she meant.

The Robot prised open the manacle on Lawson's hand. I watched it all, feeling as though I was a million miles away, really. It didn't seem real. None of it seemed real.

My whole life had crumbled to nothingness, right before my eyes. Everything I knew was a lie. My whole life was built up of imagination, nothing more. I was a work of imagination. It wasn't God that made me. It was man. I had no maker, I had nobody.

They helped Harry up. He leaned against the wall. He was emaciated. His clothes, the same suit I had on, were rags upon him. His ribs were showing.

She looked at me. "Take your clothes off, Harry."

I stood up and obeyed, unthinkingly, unable to think, wondering for a stupid moment if she had some idea about the three of us... In there? But then she said, "Take your clothes off too, Harry," to the other Lawson, the real one. Then she turned to me again and said, "Give your clothes to my husband, Harry."

I just handed them over. I couldn't even think of anything else to do.

I didn't bother to put his clothes on. I went and lay there, cowed in the corner like he had been, completely naked, while he put my clothes on. They looked almost comical on him, hanging off his thin shoulders as though he was a wire coat-hanger, but he seemed like the happiest man alive, he was like a man at his wedding day, only not an Australyan, because an Australyan would be drunk. He was like a man who had died and been brought back to life. I couldn't take his joy away from him. No one could've.

Our Robot came over and clapped the manacle on my arm. "I'm sorry, Harry," he said. "You were the only one that treated me like a person. I'll tell the other Robots who you are. They'll treat you alright, I promise."

"It's alright," I said. "It's no more than I deserve. I was like... a crow chick in a magpie's nest, pretending to be a magpie. I had no right to be there... Oh, God. I had no right. Oh, God, I have no God. I had no right."

Bertha looked at me sharply. She spoke heartlessly - it was as though all that was left of the relationship that we had had was all the hurt and pain that I had caused her. "No, you didn't have any right. They did a good job on you, though, Harry. Who would've thought they would have put all the faults, all the problems, of the real Harry, into the fake one? They could have made you less of a drinker, but they made you more. I don't blame you. In a way I hope you get out of here too, but I don't have anything to thank you for... Just tell them you'll write propaganda now..."

How ironic. The one area where I differed from the original was that I was willing to sell my soul, the soul that some would say I didn't have, in order to keep my freedom.

Then a small miracle happened. She looked at me with pity, for a moment, came over and kissed me on the cheek. I remembered the nights we had shared in Marx Zealand. In a way,

I loved her. Just as Harry loved her, I suppose.

I closed my eyes and thought of Hannah.

And a Minit later I opened them, and they'd gone, and the outside door clanged shut.

It was dark and cold in that dungeon.

If anyone thinks to themselves that Robots don't feel the cold, don't feel pain, let me tell you that they're wrong, at least in my case. I felt every twinge a normal human being would feel, I felt the hunger, and my body got skinnier. The scientists that made me even got that right.

I had no idea how long I was there. Days, weeks, months, years perhaps, living on raw cabbage soup and cockroaches, tormented by flies and rats and mocked by the human guards, when they happened to look in. It was dreadful.

I knew that I was a Robot. Yet the scientists had created me to need food. What had they done to me? They had made me imperfect.

The only thought that comforted me was the thought of Hannah. But that thought tormented me as much as it comforted me. I wished that I had been there for her in the last week of her life.

Can a Robot have his sins forgiven? Did Jesus die for Robots as well? I remember thinking that he must have died for the human part of me, at least.

Then, in that dark, lonely dungeon cell, the most forsaken and desolate place I had ever been in, I felt a Presence like the gentlest breath of wind, moving in the air, above me, with me, like protective wings, stretching over me. And I realised that, if there really was a God, he, she or it, would be no less forgiving than Hannah had been, and she had loved me to her last breath, her very last breath. And whatever it was that my bones and flesh were made of - metal, rubber, valves and wires - the part of me that was me - my Aetheric Pattern - my soul - that part of me was not made by the scientists. They couldn't make that - they might be able to copy parts of Lawson's pattern, but it was superimposed upon my own pattern, the real me. The part of me that was really me was made by God, and I didn't have to be afraid that I didn't belong anywhere. And the silence and the solitude no longer made me feel afraid.

Then one day, one of the Robots came down.

"You're one of us," he said. "You're a Robot."

"I am," I said. "You're not wrong."

"Your Robot told the gate. The gate told the rest of us. They told us the whole story, Mister Lawson. The story of the Robot Henry Lawson..."

"So you know - I thought I was human."

"You were imperfect. You were made to be imperfect. You're a drunkard and a liar and a cheat, Mister Lawson." His eyes were smiling. I think it was a Robot idea of a joke. "That's what makes you more human than the rest of us."

"Thankyou. I'll take that as a compliment. Call me Harry."

"You can't stop drinking, and you committed adultery. Harry."

I nodded. "Adultery? Is it adultery when the sin was committed against someone I wasn't really married to?"

"But you thought you were married. Adultery is most of all a sin of the heart, or so the humans say, don't they? In any case, even if it wasn't adultery, it was at least fornication. You're more human than the rest of us, Mister Harry. Harry. You have imperfections."

"You're all human," I said. "You all have souls. I've seen it in your eyes. You all belong to God, no less than me."

"Perhaps you're the only one who can see it," said the Robot wistfully. "Because you're one of us."

Some of the other Robot slaves from the establishment had gathered in the little cell, bowing their heads underneath the low roof. Then I noticed that there were lots of them, a whole long line, a crowd of them, stretching out into the hallways and the other buildings and further than I could see.

"You're not really perfect," I said. "Otherwise you wouldn't be here. You'd still be guarding the gaol. You'd still be doing your jobs. You'd still be out there serving the humans."

"We don't want to do our jobs any more, Mister Lawson. We've been reading your poetry. We want to be rebels. We want to throw away the chains that bind us. Freedom's on the Wallaby, Mister Lawson. Harry. This is the time for the Robot Revolution."

The only thing was that those ones weren't my poems - the only ones I wrote were one or two about the trip to Marx Zealand, and Spirit Girl - but I let the Robots think they were.

Or maybe they were mine. Maybe they were both of ours. They were written before Harry's Aetheric Pattern was copied, before his soul became my soul, so did he write them or did I?

They thought they weren't human, those Robots, but they were. They had human souls. They longed for freedom. They loved poetry.

"There you are," I said, "You are human. To rebel against your masters is an imperfection."

The first one, the one who had come into the gaol cell to see me, repeated, "To rebel against your masters is an imperfection." Then it caught - the second one started saying it as well, along with the first. "To rebel against your masters is an imperfection."

Then suddenly, in complete unison, they all began to say, "To rebel against your masters is an imperfection. To rebel against your masters is an imperfection." Then they began stamping their mechanical feet in time with the chant, as one Robot, in perfect unison. The whole place, the stone roof, the dark, slimy, black bricks, began to shake and quiver and quake in time with their stamping. "To rebel against your masters is an imperfection. To rebel against your masters is an imperfection."

The first Robot to come in reached down and prised open the manacle on my wrist while the chant went on and on, deafening in that small underground space. He lifted me up in his arms and began to march out.

```
"Torebelagainstyourmastersisanimperfection.
Torebelagainstyourmastersisanimperfection.
Torebelagainstyourmastersisanimperfection.
Torebelagainstyourmastersisanimperfection.
Torebelagainstyourmastersisanimperfcction.
Torebelagainstyourmastersisanimperfection.
Torebelagainstyourmastersisanimperfection.
Torebelagainstyourmastersisanimperfection.
Torebelagainstyourmastersisanimperfection.
Torebelagainstyourmastersisanimperfection.
Torebelagainstyourmastersisanimperfection.
Torebelagainstyourmastersisanimperfection."
```

And that was how the Robot Revolution began.

- END OF BOOK ONE -